Animal Instincts

Diamondback saw his mistake too late. He clawed for his six-gun as he tried to reach the fence, but Gassy's mule caught and bit him in the back of the neck. Diamondback screamed and dove through the rails, probably saving his life. When he got clear of the corral, the man was in such a fit of pain and rage that he drew his gun and started to shoot Moses.

"No!" Longarm shouted, reaching for his own gun as Diamondback's first bullet went wide of its mark and the mule took off running.

Gassy fired just an instant later and his aim was true. Longarm saw Diamondback's mouth fly open as he struck the fence. Gassy shot him a second time in the back and the thief toppled headfirst through the railing to hang there with his legs on one side of the pole corral, and his head and arms on the other side.

"Dammit, Gassy, you killed him," Longarm swore.

"Yep."

Gassy went to Diamondback and grabbed the man's boots. He farted, then pulled Diamondback out from between the rails and spit a stream of tobacco juice in the dead man's face. "This son of a bitch shot me and then was going to shoot Moses! He deserved what he got."

DON'T MISS THESE
ALL-ACTION WESTERN SERIES
FROM THE BERKLEY PUBLISHING GROUP

THE GUNSMITH by J. R. Roberts
Clint Adams was a legend among lawmen, outlaws, and ladies. They called him . . . the Gunsmith.

LONGARM by Tabor Evans
The popular long-running series about Deputy U.S. Marshal Long—his life, his loves, his fight for justice.

SLOCUM by Jake Logan
Today's longest-running action Western. John Slocum rides a deadly trail of hot blood and cold steel.

BUSHWHACKERS by B. J. Lanagan
An action-packed series by the creators of Longarm! The rousing adventures of the most brutal gang of cutthroats ever assembled—Quantrill's Raiders.

DIAMONDBACK by Guy Brewer
Dex Yancey is Diamondback, a Southern gentleman turned con man when his brother cheats him out of the family fortune. Ladies love him. Gamblers hate him. But nobody pulls one over on Dex . . .

WILDGUN by Jack Hanson
The blazing adventures of mountain man Will Barlow—from the creators of Longarm!

TEXAS TRACKER by Tom Calhoun
Meet J.T. Law: the most relentless—and dangerous—manhunter in all Texas. Where sheriffs and posses fail, he's the best man to bring in the most vicious outlaws—for a price.

TABOR EVANS

LONGARM

AND THE APACHE WAR

JOVE BOOKS, NEW YORK

THE BERKLEY PUBLISHING GROUP
Published by the Penguin Group
Penguin Group (USA) Inc.
375 Hudson Street, New York, New York 10014, USA

Penguin Group (Canada), 90 Eglinton Avenue East, Suite 700, Toronto, Ontario M4P 2Y3, Canada
(a division of Pearson Penguin Canada Inc.)
Penguin Books Ltd., 80 Strand, London WC2R 0RL, England
Penguin Group Ireland, 25 St. Stephen's Green, Dublin 2, Ireland (a division of Penguin Books Ltd.)
Penguin Group (Australia), 250 Camberwell Road, Camberwell, Victoria 3124, Australia
(a division of Pearson Australia Group Pty. Ltd.)
Penguin Books India Pvt. Ltd., 11 Community Centre, Panchsheel Park, New Delhi—110 017, India
Penguin Group (NZ), Cnr. Airborne and Rosedale Roads, Albany, Auckland 1310, New Zealand
(a division of Pearson New Zealand Ltd.)
Penguin Books (South Africa) (Pty.) Ltd., 24 Sturdee Avenue, Rosebank, Johannesburg 2196,
South Africa

Penguin Books Ltd., Registered Offices: 80 Strand, London WC2R 0RL, England

LONGARM AND THE APACHE WAR

A Jove Book / published by arrangement with the author

PRINTING HISTORY
Jove edition / May 2006

ISBN: 0-515-14130-5

JOVE®
Jove Books are published by The Berkley Publishing Group,
a division of Penguin Group (USA) Inc.,
375 Hudson Street, New York, New York 10014.
JOVE is a registered trademark of Penguin Group (USA) Inc.
The "J" design is a trademark belonging to Penguin Group (USA) Inc.

PRINTED IN THE UNITED STATES OF AMERICA

10 9 8 7 6 5 4 3 2 1

Chapter 1

Deputy United States Marshal Custis Long stood drinking an early morning cup of coffee beside the window of his Denver apartment and watched people passing by in the street below. It was a warm day in May and there were thunderheads hanging over the Rocky Mountains, which usually meant that it would rain that afternoon. Longarm didn't mind that a bit. The previous winter had been disappointing in terms of snowfall. He could see the distant peaks to the west and most of them were already devoid of snow while nearby Cherry Creek was hardly more than a trickle. Without good summer rains, the town and surrounding farms and ranches would be bone-dry and hurting by autumn. Longarm had seen prairie fires before and knew that they could travel for miles if blown by wind across dry grasslands. These fires had wiped out farms in the past and they could well do it again this summer if the rains failed.

But on this bright spring morning, the world seemed right and so he turned away from his window and prepared to finish dressing and then go to his office at the downtown federal building. He went over to his mirror and picked up a small pair of scissors which he used to trim his thick handlebar mustache. Satisfied, he slipped on his vest and then his brown tweed suit coat. He added a shoestring tie and topped himself off with an expensive Stetson with a stylish flat crown.

Longarm also made sure that his hideout derringer was in good working order. The derringer was one of his favorite weapons and it had saved his life on several occasions. It was a .44 caliber with twin barrels and it replaced the customary watch fob attached to a gold chain and his Ingersol railroad watch. By this means he could appear to be fiddling, with his timepiece when he was instead drawing the dangerous little pistol. And while the derringer had a very short range of accuracy, it was perfect for sudden and deadly confrontations at close quarters in a saloon.

Longarm righted his Stetson at just the proper angle and was satisfied with his appearance. He stood about six-foot-four and weighed just over two hundred pounds which made him a standout in any crowd. Despite his obvious physical strength, Longarm was by nature a quiet, introspective man who preferred not to bring attention to himself. In fact, he did not even wear his federal marshal's badge openly and his Colt revolver, which he wore on his left hip butt forward, was kept partially concealed under his coat.

Longarm put the mustache scissors aside, drained his cup of strong black coffee and checked his pocket watch. It was twenty minutes until eight and that meant it was time to leave for the federal office.

He locked his door and was about to move down the hallway toward the lobby when he heard a woman scream from one of the apartments. Longarm paused for a moment and then he heard the woman scream a second time.

"Damn," he muttered, "it's Lucy Dooley and her drunken husband fighting again."

Jasper Dooley was a bartender at one of the all night saloons downtown. Sober until six A.M. when he ended his night shift he would toss down four or five stiff shots of whiskey before leaving work for his apartment. And while the man could probably have handled that much whiskey before tumbling into his bed, he often stopped at several other saloons and tossed down a few more whiskies just for good measure. There were times when Dooley was so drunk by the time he got home to his pretty young wife that the man had to practically be carried to bed. When that was necessary, Jasper became very combative. Longarm knew this because he had helped Lucy wrestle Jasper into their apartment on more than one occasion.

When Lucy screamed a third time Longarm also heard a loud smacking sound and knew that Jasper was getting rough with his wife, who was about half his size.

Longarm hated to become involved in domestic squabbles, but he simply could not tolerate a bully and that was exactly what Jasper Dooley created in himself after an early morning of hard drinking. So Longarm marched down the hallway to their apartment door and knocked loudly.

"Help!" Lucy screamed.

Longarm didn't bother to wait for the door to be opened. He expected it to be unlocked so he turned the knob and pushed inside just in time to see Jasper kneeling over his wife with a raised fist. Lucy Dooley had her hands over her face trying to protect herself from any more blows, but Longarm could see that her pretty face was already bloodied.

3

"Dammit, Jasper!" Longarm shouted, rushing across the apartment to grab the husband's upraised fist. "This time you've gone way too far!"

Jasper shifted his close-set, bloodshot eyes onto Longarm and hissed, "Marshal, get the hell out of my apartment!"

Longarm had a grip like a blacksmith's vise and he used it now to corkscrew Jasper's wrist far back until the man cried out in pain and his fingers splayed. Then Longarm pulled the big man off his small, comely wife and slapped him back and forth across his face until blood ran from Jasper's smashed lips. Longarm grabbed the drunken bully by his lapels and propelled him to his feet. "Jasper, you sorry bastard, his time you're going to jail for wife beating!"

But Lucy crawled to her feet and tried to pull her husband free of Longarm's grasp. "It's all right," she gasped. "I'm going to be all right."

"You're hurt," he said. "Your face is already starting to swell. Lucy, there's no need to put up with this kind of treatment until Jasper finally beats your brains to mush! I'll see that he goes to jail for at least a month this time."

"No, please," Lucy begged. "Jasper needs to keep his job."

Longarm had heard this kind of talk from desperate and dependent women before and he had no time or patience for it. "Jasper is going to lose his job anyway because of his drinking. And you don't need a man who's going to kill you someday in a drunken rage."

But Lucy wasn't listening. Her lower lip was lacerated and one of her eyes was already starting to swell closed, but she continued begging Longarm to let her husband off one more time.

4

"He won't do it ever again. Will you Jasper?"

Jasper's eyes were starting to roll up in his head and he looked ready to pass out drunk. "Naw," he muttered. "Bad night. Bad night and won't do it again."

"See!" Lucy cried, trying to force hope into her voice. "My poor husband has had a *real* bad night. That saloon where he works is a terrible place. You don't know how much truck he has to put up with every night. It's why he has to have a few drinks to unwind after his shift. Please, Custis, let him go. I'll take care of him."

Longarm knew he was making a mistake, but since Lucy was unwilling to press charges of assault and battery against this drunken bully there really wasn't much point in taking Jasper to the city jail.

"All right," he said, throwing Jasper backward so that the drunk's head bounced against the wall. He grabbed the man by his throat and squeezed it until he had the man's full attention. "If you ever hit your wife like this again, Jasper, I'm going to beat you to a bloody pulp and then make sure you go straight to jail no matter what she wants. Do you understand me?"

Jasper tried to spit into Longarm's face, but couldn't work it up. Disgusted and filled with rage, Longarm drove a powerful uppercut into Jasper's stomach then hit the man as he was sliding down the wall with a right hook that knocked him out cold.

"Custis, you might have killed him!" Lucy cried, kneeling beside her husband.

"Yeah, and then I might have saved your life." Longarm rubbed his stinging knuckles. "Lucy, when are you going to wake up and leave this rotten son of a bitch?"

Her lower lip trembled and she fought back tears. "I can't."

"Why, because of the money he makes? Why I bet Jasper drinks up half of his wages every morning."

She began to cry so Longarm grabbed the unconscious bartender by the arm and hauled him to his bed. He lifted Jasper up and dumped him facedown on the bedspread then turned back to Lucy. "You've got to leave him, girl. He's going to beat you to death some morning."

"I'm expecting his child!" Lucy blurted.

Longarm groaned. "And he's still knocking you around like this?"

She only stood about five feet tall and couldn't have weighed more than ninety pounds. Now, with her face smeared with blood and puffing up fast, she reminded Longarm of a scared little schoolgirl. Pretty, but terrified. That was how he thought of little Miss Lucy Dooley. "I ain't told Jasper yet."

"Why not?"

She sobbed. "Because he doesn't *want* children."

"Damn," Longarm whispered, shaking his head. "So do you think him finding out you are pregnant is going to improve this miserable situation?"

"I don't know what to think or do."

Longarm licked blood from his knuckles. "You are about out of choices on this, Lucy. Most of your choices are real bad. The only right thing to do is to leave him and go back to your family."

"They don't want me. They . . ."

Lucy couldn't finish. She threw herself against Longarm, hugged him with all her might and cried. When he finally got her to let go and calm down he said, "Where is your family?"

6

"In Flagstaff, Arizona. My father works for the railroad. My mother works at a diner. They haven't got much money either."

"Well," Longarm said, "they might not want the responsibility of you and your baby, but folks generally do the right thing by their children and grandchildren. If I were you, Lucy, I'd leave for Arizona today while that worthless husband of yours is still out cold."

"I couldn't even if I wanted to because I've no travel money."

"I'll give it to you," he said without hesitation. "Lucy, I'll give you enough to get to Arizona where you can start over fresh."

She shook her head as if he were talking like a fool. "With a baby and no husband?"

Longarm could see her point, but argued, "Girl, if anybody asks, including your parents, tell them that your husband died."

"But that'd be a lie!"

"So is your marriage," he said bluntly. "And this life you're living. You deserve better. So does the child you're bearing. Are you sure that you're pregnant?"

"Pretty sure."

"Well, maybe you're not."

"And maybe I am." Lucy gazed through her tears into the little bedroom at her unconscious husband. "Jasper always vowed that he'd kill me if I ever tried to leave him."

"There's a train heading out of Denver in less than four hours. Jasper won't wake up that soon. You'll be on the train and miles away before he comes around."

She scrubbed away tears and blood with her sleeve and Longarm could see that she was giving the matter

7

some serious consideration. "Do it, Lucy. I'm giving you your best chance."

"But Jasper knows I'm from Arizona."

"Lucy, I don't want to hurt your feelings any more than they've already been hurt today, but I seriously doubt that your husband cares enough to come after you."

Fresh tears welled up in her eyes. "He doesn't?"

"I'm sorry, but no."

Longarm surveyed the little apartment. It was depressing. This young couple had no furniture except what Lucy had found discarded in alleys and down along Cherry Creek. Furniture so broken and worn that even the city's hobos didn't want it.

"You can't do any worse for yourself and your baby than this," Longarm said, taking out his wallet. "Damn, I'm short on cash today. I'll have to go to the bank. Meet me at noon at the train station."

She swallowed hard and seemed unable to make a decision.

"Lucy, if you don't take my offer, he's going to beat you to death before that baby ever sees the light of day. Trust me on that. You *must* get far away from Jasper."

"I have a sister that lives in a little town outside of Flagstaff," she said almost to herself. "Claire and I were real close growing up. She's married with three boys, but she's good-hearted and I think that she'd help me."

"Fine," Longarm said, replacing his wallet. "Meet me at the train station. I'll have a one-way ticket to Flagstaff and some extra cash for you to get to your sister."

Lucy finally dipped her chin. "All right. Noon at the train station."

8

Longarm gently patted the little woman on top of her head which didn't even come to his shoulder. "Lucy, I'd feel a lot easier if you were out of this apartment in the next hour. Just pack up what you can carry in a bag or satchel and leave. Will you do that?"

"Yes."

"All right then," he said. "I'll see you at noon."

Longarm was late for work so he hurried up West Colfax. Near the U.S. Mint at Cherokee and Colfax he turned into the United States federal building. He would check in at his office just to make sure that there was no trouble and then he would hurry off to withdraw Lucy's traveling money and meet her at the train station. There wasn't a lot of time to spare, but Longarm was confident that he'd get there by noon and then he'd make sure that poor girl was on the train and heading out of Colorado. As for the possibility that Jasper Dooley might actually try to follow his young wife to Arizona . . . well, Longarm would have a talk with that drunken bully and make sure that Dooley never tried to find his wife. As far as Longarm was concerned it was best if Jasper never knew that he had fathered a child.

Chapter 2

"Custis!" Marshal Billy Vail called as Longarm strode past his boss's office. "Where the hell have you been?"

Longarm stopped and backed up a pace. "What do you mean?"

"It's eight-thirty and I've been waiting for you."

Longarm removed his hat and ambled into Billy's office. They were friends and Billy wasn't usually so abrupt and tense. "What's the problem?"

"Sit down and I'll explain, but it will take some time."

"I'm in kind of a hurry this morning," Longarm told the man. "Can you tell it to me fast?"

"No."

"Try," Longarm urged.

Billy gave Longarm a disapproving glance and then went to sit in his big office chair behind an enormous oak desk. The marshal took a deep breath and said, "I'm afraid that all hell is breaking loose down by the San Carlos Apache Reservation."

"Sounds bad."

"It is."

Longarm folded his arms across his chest. "Care to elaborate?"

Billy grabbed his favorite pipe and reamed it out. He jammed in a fresh load of tobacco, fired up the briar and blew a large cloud of smoke over Longarm's head. "There's an Apache war going on down in the middle of Arizona and the secretary of indian lands wants a full and honest report."

"Have we got another Geronimo or Cochise on our hands?"

"No," Billy answered, "I'm afraid this war is far more complex. The long and the short of it is that the conflict is all about water rights."

"Water rights?"

"Custis, are you familiar with that part of the southwest that takes in the San Carlos Indian Reservation?"

He considered the question a moment. "I know that the San Carlos is located in the eastern part of Arizona and that those Apache are still tough and independent fighters."

"That's true," Billy said, puffing rapidly on his pipe. "Let me lay out for you as simply and as straightforward as I possibly can what the problem is down on the San Carlos. Provided, that is, that you have the time."

"Stow it, Billy. It's just that I have something important to do before noon."

"And you don't think that what I'm going to tell you is important?" Billy looked upset. Before Longarm could summon up some words of appeasement, the man added, "Custis, if you're not up for this assignment, I guarantee you that I'll find an adequate replacement. Possibly Deputy Purvis Potter. He's been itching to get out in the field."

Longarm scoffed outright. "Potter is so inept he couldn't find his butt with his own right hand. And you know he'll just mess up. Most likely get himself shot or scalped."

"Potter is a sworn officer of the law," Billy argued. "Sure, he does tend to get a little rattled under pressure, but . . ."

Longarm extracted his pocket watch and frowned. "Billy, we're wasting time. Tell me about the Apache and their water problem."

"It's fairly simple," Billy said. "Out in Arizona, water is everything. It's more valuable than gold. Whoever controls the water controls the power in that desert country."

"I understand that," Longarm said, wishing his boss would get right to the crux of the matter.

"So here's the deal," Billy said, puffing faster. "The north of the San Carlos Indian Reservation is fed by a very good source of water called Canyon Creek. Canyon Creek, as I've been told, runs directly through a big canyon to the north of the reservation then is used on irrigated Apache fields and farms."

Longarm wasn't sure that he'd heard his boss correctly. "Did you say that the San Carlos Apache are *farming*?"

"And raising livestock," Billy said.

Longarm shook his head. "I never thought I'd see the day when an Apache would use a hoe for anything other than splitting a white man's scalp."

"Well," Billy said, "when they were relocated they took the reservation that they were assigned and had no choice but to start farming. Either they did that or they'd starve on the meager government rations. And I've heard that they've made a pretty good go especially with corn and beans and hay which they both use and sell."

"What kind of livestock are they raising down there?"

"Cattle, sheep and horses."

"They love roasting horsemeat," Longarm observed.

"That's really beside the point, isn't it?" Billy had to relight his pipe. When he got the thing smoking again, he continued. "The point, Custis, is that they desperately need Canyon Creek's water. Without it their ranches and farms will dry up and blow away."

"So who is trying to take their water?" Longarm asked, figuring he already knew the answer.

"I'm afraid it's the same old story. Just north of the San Carlos Reservation there is a small gold strike underway."

"Gold strikes are *never* small, Billy."

"I suppose not. The boomtown that is causing the trouble is named Canyon City."

"So why can't the miners and businessmen in Canyon City simply use the water that passes through their boomtown and let it keep flowing onto the reservation?"

"Because they want to divert Canyon Creek *around* the San Carlos Reservation."

Longarm shook his head. "How the hell can they justify that?"

Billy shrugged. "It seems that the original streambed didn't flow onto the reservation. The miners claim the Apache diverted it just before the treaty that gave them the reservation. They swear that the stream was never meant to flow on the reservation and that they're just diverting it to its original water course."

14

Longarm shook his head in utter amazement. "How convenient for the miners and citizens of Canyon City."

"Yes, isn't it, though," Billy agreed.

"Their claim will never stand up in court."

"Probably not," Billy agreed, "but a court battle could drag on for years while the San Carlos Apache starve because their fields dry up and blow away and their livestock die of thirst. So you see, either way, they'd lose."

"They're up against another stacked deck, huh?"

"I'm afraid so," Billy agreed. "Especially since it appears that the miners have a number of powerful allies on their side."

Longarm shook his head. "So, who have the miners bribed?"

Billy stopped puffing his pipe. "That is not completely clear yet, but I think we can assume it is someone very powerful and influential back in Washington."

Longarm snorted. "Another corrupt bureaucrat."

"Regrettably, that appears to be so," Billy said. "But that's not our concern. What we need to do is to make sure that blood is not shed until we find a way to help the Apache receive justice. Otherwise, they'll suffer terribly."

"Have the people of Canyon City already diverted the stream?"

"I don't know."

Longarm sat back thinking the San Carlos dispute sounded like a powder keg with a short fuse. "And you want me to go to Arizona."

"Right now. Today."

"And try to keep the Apache and the miners from killing each other?"

"Absolutely."

Billy stood up and handed Longarm a manila envelope. "Here is your train ticket and travel money. Good luck."

"Thanks a lot," Longarm muttered as he came out of his chair and headed for the door.

"Oh, Custis?"

"Yeah?"

"Don't get scalped or ambushed. Most likely both sides of the trouble will want you dead."

Longarm cussed under his breath as he went out the door.

Chapter 3

Longarm had very little time to prepare for his train journey to Arizona. He went back to his apartment, packed and then and stopped at Lucy Dooley's door on his way out of the building. He rapped softly on the door and when there was no answer he decided to go on about his own business rather than risk waking up Jasper. With any luck that mean drunk would be moved out by the time that Longarm returned to Denver.

He was running late by the time he arrived at the train depot, but Lucy was waiting for him just as she'd promised. Longarm gave her a one-way ticket to Flagstaff along with some travel money he'd withdrawn from his personal bank account.

"Custis, why are you carrying bags?" she asked as she prepared to board the train.

"You won't believe this, Lucy, but I've just got an assignment out in Arizona."

She brightened. "*Where* in Arizona?"

"It has to do with the San Carlos Apache Reservation."

Lucy shrugged her shoulders. "Is that anywhere near Flagstaff?"

"South of it," Longarm said, hearing the engineer blow the steam whistle signaling that the train was about to depart. "Lucy, it looks as if we'll be traveling all the way to Arizona together."

Lucy didn't even try to hide her delight at this news, but when she smiled, her cut lip reopened and bled. Longarm used his handkerchief to dab away the blood, then he helped the young woman board the train.

"Damn that Jasper," he muttered, folding his blood-stained handkerchief and putting it back in his pocket. "If I never see the man again it will be too damn soon."

"Amen," Lucy said, breathing a sigh of relief. "I am glad to be leaving, but scared nearly to death that Jasper will track me down and kill me in Arizona."

"He won't ever have enough money to buy a train ticket," Longarm told her. "Don't worry about Jasper."

"I'll try not to," she said even as her eyes scanned the crowd gathered on the train platform. "But he is a vengeful man. When he discovers that I've left him he will go crazy with anger."

Longarm was sure that was true. "If Jasper makes any attempt to come after you I'll take care of him so that he never bothers anyone again."

The conductor punched their tickets and gave them directions. Lucy was in the second coach traveling in her own sleeping compartment while Longarm was in the third coach.

"I haven't traveled anywhere in years," she nervously confided as they stood in the aisle listening to the train whistle. "I'm nervous."

"You'll be fine," he promised as he carried her frayed little valise into her compartment. "These

18

doors lock and I'm in compartment three-B in the very next car if you need anything."

"Can we eat together and visit often?" she asked hopefully.

Longarm gave her a hug. Lucy looked like hell with her black eye, swollen face and split lip. But by the time they reached Arizona she'd be looking and feeling a whole lot better. Why, as pretty as she'd be when she healed, Lucy would have more men courting her than she could shake a stick at despite being pregnant. Longarm just hoped she'd use better judgment before she chose her next mate.

"Can we meet for supper?" she asked.

"Sure," he said, removing his pocket watch. "I'll be by to check on you in a few hours. Until then, you need to rest."

"I will," she told him.

Longarm left her then and went to his own cramped sleeping compartment. Their train would be heading south to Pueblo on the Denver and Rio Grand Railroad where it would hook up with the Santa Fe that would take them all the way to Arizona. It was a long, but scenic ride and he was pretty sure that Lucy would soon relax and begin to enjoy herself as she contemplated a much happier future than she'd ever had with her violent husband.

Longarm sat down in his compartment and extracted a cigar from his coat pocket. He stared out the window at the last of the passengers hurrying to board the train and tried to put his own mind at ease. He'd stuck his neck out pretty far by encouraging Miss Dooley to flee her husband. If things went bad for her in Flagstaff he would be partially responsible. But Longarm couldn't imagine things ever being any worse for Lucy than they had been in Denver. And he told himself that if he had not intervened on Lucy's behalf, Jasper would have soon beaten his wife to death and, unwittingly, his own unborn child.

"So I've saved two lives," he said aloud to himself as he lit his cigar and waited for the train to leave the station.

Longarm's eyes were drooping when the train jolted into motion. He opened his eyes just in time to see Jasper running for the train. Longarm couldn't believe it! He watched in astonishment as Jasper leapt onto the slowly moving train and vanished into the second car.

The man was after his wife! Somehow, he'd awakened and learned of Lucy's plan to escape him forever. And now, still drunk and consumed by boundless fury and a sense of betrayal, Jasper was going to claim his wife even if that meant taking her by the throat and throwing her off the train.

Or worse.

Longarm surged out of his seat and bolted through the compartment door. He collided in the aisle with a heavy-set woman and knocked her ass over tea kettle. She screamed at him, but Longarm didn't have time to apologize. He drew his gun as he charged between the coaches and entered the second railroad car to find it in a state of pure chaos.

Jasper was kicking and pounding at the locked door of his wife's compartment. A young train employee who had tried to restrain him was lying in the aisle with blood pouring down his face.

"Jasper!" Longarm shouted as he tried to push his way through the crush of panicked passengers.

Jasper heard and recognized Longarm's voice. He

drew a gun from under his coat and grabbed a boy, drawing him close. "Marshal Long," he shouted as women screamed in terror. "*You* put Lucy up to this!"

Longarm had to try and reason with Jasper in order to keep the man from harming the boy or someone else in this crowded coach. "Put the boy down and drop your gun," he ordered. "You're already in deep trouble, but not so deep that you can't get out of this with jail time."

"I ain't going to jail," Jasper hissed, pointing the six-gun at the squirming boy's head. "And you're the one that had better drop the gun right now or I'll splatter this brat's brains all over this coach."

Longarm knew that Jasper wasn't running a bluff. He had seen desperate men before and they could not be pushed over the edge of their tottering sanity or they would kill indiscriminately and without hesitation.

"All right," he said, pitching his six-gun onto a seat. "Just let the boy go and get off this train."

"Not without my wife!"

"Listen, Jasper . . ."

"Shut up!" Jasper screamed. "You're the one that is takin' her away from me. You've always had eyes for my Lucy and now you think she's just going to run away from me so you can have her. Well, lawman, you're dead wrong!"

Longarm saw that Jasper was going to topple over into the abyss. That the drunken and rejected man was going to shoot him and that there wasn't much of a chance of stopping that from happening.

And as if he had read Longarm's mind, Jasper cocked back the hammer of his gun and shouted, "Lucy, I know you're hiding in there. Don't you want to see me blow Custis Long's head off?"

"Please!" Lucy wailed, her voice carrying through the door of her compartment. "Don't hurt anyone."

"Then unlock your door and come out!"

Longarm saw the doorknob to her compartment turn and he held his breath just hoping that Jasper would take his eyes off him and offer an opportunity. But Jasper's full attention remained riveted on Longarm and his finger was pressing tight on the trigger.

Suddenly, Lucy threw open the door and hurled her small body at Jasper catching her husband by surprise. Jasper was a big man, but Lucy hit him just as the train lurched and they both fell over sideways.

It was all the break that Longarm needed. He snatched his gun up and took aim just as Jasper was struggling to free himself from Lucy. They fired at almost the same instant.

Jasper's bullet lightly grazed Longarm's shoulder. Longarm's bullet smashed into the drunk's throat, ripping it apart. Jasper fell back on a seat as the other passengers went into hysterics. Longarm shot Jasper a second time in the chest and the retort of his gun was so loud in the coach that it was deafening.

It was over. Women were howling and children were screeching, but Longarm didn't care as he rushed over to Lucy and pulled her away from her twitching husband. Lucy was as white as a ghost and trembling like a leaf as Longarm eased her back into her compartment and shut the door behind them so he could hold her in private and calm her down.

"It's finished," he said, still hearing screams outside the little compartment. "He'll never hurt you again. You saved my life out there, Lucy. If you hadn't thrown yourself at him, he'd have shot me where I stood and probably would have killed some passengers to boot."

"Yes," she whispered, "Jasper would have gone down fighting. He'd have shot up the door to my compartment and killed me rather than leave the train alone."

"I've got to go out there and get things under control," Longarm told the young woman as they both listened to the screaming passengers.

"Don't leave me yet."

"I have to, but I'll be back soon. Just lie down and be still. Everything will be fine from now on."

"Do you promise?"

Longarm had no right to promise this brave and badly abused woman anything, but he did it anyway. And then he left her and went back out into the aisle. The train was already a mile south of the train station, but it would have to be stopped and Jasper's body removed. There would, of course, be a report of the killing to fill out and many delays.

"Oh, hell," Longarm muttered to himself. "Jasper isn't worth all the bother. I'll just pitch his worthless carcass off the train and send a telegram back to the authorities explaining things when I get to the train station down in Pueblo."

The conductor was a white haired gentleman in his sixties. "Marshal Long, I'll have to stop this train," he said, draping his coat over the body.

"No, you won't," Longarm told the man. "Just get these passengers settled down and I'll take care of this body."

"But . . ."

"Do it," Longarm said with an edge in his voice.

23

"All right, Marshal. It's your call and your responsibility."

"Damn right it is."

Longarm turned and studied the faces of the shocked and horrified passengers. Then without a word he grabbed Jasper with care so as not to let the dead man's fresh blood ruin his own suit. He lifted the body and dragged it down the aisle until he came to the door between the coaches. Pushing it open he dragged Jasper out onto the open platform and then shoved him off the train. Jasper bounced like a child's rag doll and then lay still beside the tracks.

Longarm used his already soiled handkerchief to wipe a few drops of Jasper's blood from his hands. He stared back down the train tracks as Jasper's remains grew small in the fading distance.

With luck, someone would find the body and remove it before a pack of stray dogs found it first.

Chapter 4

It took a while for the passengers in Lucy's coach to calm down. Longarm went back to his own compartment and cleaned the bullet wound that had creased his shoulder. The wound was hardly more than a scratch, but it hurt like hell and had bled considerably, ruining both his shirt and coat. He would have to buy replacements when the train reached Pueblo. Longarm wasn't happy about having to spend the money, but he felt lucky that he had not been killed when he remembered that he and Jasper had fired almost at the same instant. If Jasper's aim had been a little better they both might be dead.

Longarm was sipping good whiskey from a silver flask while struggling to bandage the wound on his shoulder when there was soft knock on his door. "Who is it?"

"The conductor. Marshal, may I please have a word with you?"

Longarm opened the door. "What can I do for you?"

The conductor shifted his feet to the rocking of the

train and cleared his voice. "The passengers are pretty upset over what happened up in the next coach."

"And I can't say as I blame them. What happened wasn't pretty."

"No, it wasn't. And they'd like me to assure them that there won't be any more shooting or killing."

"There won't be," Longarm promised. "The man that opened fire was a jealous and crazy husband. He was a loose cannon and you can tell the passengers that I regret the . . . the danger that they were placed in during the gunfight. However, there was no way that it could have been avoided."

"Marshal, they're wondering if that Mrs. Dooley has any more men coming after her."

"Absolutely not."

"They don't feel comfortable with her in the coach. I'm going to have to move her to another car. Unfortunately, all the private sleeping compartments are occupied on this run down to Pueblo. That means Mrs. Dooley either has to sit in coach . . . or I thought perhaps she could stay here with you until we get to Pueblo where we can see if there are other travel arrangements that can be made on her behalf."

"She can stay here with me and that's something I should have suggested anyway. We'll be rolling into Pueblo in what? Three hours?"

The conductor consulted his pocket watch. "That's about right."

"Please ask Mrs. Dooley to come join me."

"Yes, sir." The conductor looked very relieved and smiled with appreciation. "Mrs. Dooley is quite upset and I think being with you will be very calming."

Longarm raised his whiskey flask. "*This* is what's most calming," he told the conductor. "What the

26

young woman needs most is privacy and a strong drink."

The conductor raised his eyebrows, but did not argue the point as he closed the door.

A few minutes later Lucy appeared carrying her valise. "Thank you for letting me stay here with you until we reach Pueblo. I'm pretty upset, as you can probably imagine. Also, I wanted to see how badly you were hurt."

Longarm wasn't wearing a shirt. "It's just a flesh wound," he said, glancing at his shoulder. "But it did ruin my coat and shirt."

"Here," she offered, "let me help you bandage that. Did you put any medicine on it?"

"I washed the wound off with some good Kentucky whiskey," he answered. "That's excellent medicine both for the outside *and* the inside of a man."

"I'm sure that is sometimes the case," she told him as she helped to tie a clean handkerchief around his upper arm. "The bleeding has stopped, but I think it would be wise for you to see a doctor when we reach Pueblo."

"I don't need a doctor for a bullet scratch."

Lucy took a deep breath then blurted, "Custis, I have to know. Did you *really* toss Jasper's body off the train like a discarded piece of trash?"

"Yes."

Her face showed confusion. "But what about . . ."

"A funeral?"

"That's right. Jasper wasn't worth much, but he did deserve that much."

"That's where you and I have differing opinions," Longarm told the young widow. "Any man that beats

27

up on a woman deserves nothing. Not a burial, not a headstone, and not a parting word from the Bible."

"But Jasper is just lying out there by the tracks and . . ."

Longarm handed her the flask. "Jasper is your sad history. Put him out of your mind forever and move on," he advised. "Besides, do you have any money to give him a decent funeral?"

"You know that I don't, but . . ."

"But nothing," Longarm interrupted. "If I had kept him on board then we'd be responsible for his burial. This way we're not. And that's the way I want it. Anyway, just buying a new shirt and jacket is going to cost plenty and I haven't the funds to pay an undertaker . . . even if I wanted to. Is that understood?"

Lucy nodded and drank from the flask. She coughed, shuddered, and drank some more.

"Take it easy," he advised. "That's pretty strong stuff. Are you used to drinking?"

"No, never. Jasper always drank enough for the both of us."

"Then go easy or it will hit you hard."

Lucy nodded, but took another pull. She sat down and stared out the window at the passing landscape with tears rolling down her bruised cheeks.

"Lucy," he consoled, "it will be all right. Starting today your life will begin to change for the better."

"I hope so. But I never thought things would turn out like this. I thought when I married Jasper that we would live together until we got old and have a bunch of happy and handsome kids. Now, Jasper is gone and I'm pregnant without a husband. Custis, I haven't any idea what is waiting for me in Arizona."

"I know what's waiting for me in Arizona," he said.

"Big trouble between some greedy white miners and some damned poor and desperate Apaches. But you will do fine, Lucy."

"But what will I say when people ask about the baby?"

"You can tell everyone in perfect truth that your husband was traveling with you on this train when he was shot and killed."

A protest rose up in her throat. "But he was . . ."

Longarm silenced her with an upraised finger. "Lucy, from now on just tell people that Jasper was shot to death and that it's far too painful to go into the details. Folks will accept that and you'll have their complete sympathy. And I'll promise you something else."

She hesitated then asked, "What's that?"

"You'll have a lot of Arizona men come courting."

Her eyes widened in surprise and disbelief. "But I'll be expecting!"

"They won't care. The farther west you go the fewer women there are . . . especially young and pretty ones like yourself. Take my word for it . . . you'll be able to pick and choose from a bunch of fine young bachelors."

Lucy tipped up the flask and emptied it. "I'm not sure that I ever want to marry again. Jasper was so horrible that I fear I have no judgment when it comes to men and marriage."

"How old were you when you married Jasper?"

"Fifteen."

Longarm scoffed. "You were just a child! You're a woman now. And a beautiful one at that."

"Do you really think so?"

"I sure do."

29

Lucy smiled painfully. "Words are cheap, Custis."

"Meaning?"

Maybe it was the whiskey talking or maybe it was some desperate inner need that made her say, "I so badly need some love and reassurance. Custis, the honest truth is that I haven't been treated well for so long or given so much as a kind word that I feel like an ugly, pregnant and undesirable hag."

Longarm had to laugh out loud. "How pregnant are you? I can't even see a swelling of your body yet."

"I might be a month pregnant or even three. I don't know."

"Then I take it you've not seen a doctor yet?"

"Of course not. Who has money for doctors?"

"You recommended that I see one for this scratch and yet you don't think that you need to see a doctor about your baby?" he challenged.

"I guess I'll see one before I'm due," she said, touching her stomach.

Longarm put his arm around Lucy. "Whoever gets you and the baby you're carrying is going to be doubly blessed."

Fresh tears welled up in Lucy's eyes. "You sure know how to make a woman feel better."

"Thanks."

"So why don't we *both* make each other feel better right now."

Longarm thought that he knew what she meant, but he had to be certain. "Lucy, do you want me to . . ."

She threw her arms around his neck and kissed him hard. "Yes!"

Longarm had a moment of doubt. He'd never knowingly made love to a woman carrying a baby inside and

30

he wasn't sure that he wanted to start right now. But Lucy badly needed him to show her that she was still very desirable. If he turned her aside after she'd so freely offered herself, then he might ruin whatever little self-confidence she had left.

And he couldn't do that. Wouldn't do that.

"I'll fold these seats down into a bed," he said quietly. "And I'll be very gentle with you, Lucy."

"Don't worry," she said. "I'm small, but I'm strong. And I'll tell you if it hurts."

Longarm made the bed down and finished undressing. When he turned around to look at the woman, she was undressed and had a beautiful body. He could hardly see the small mound of her belly and Lucy's breasts were small but firm and inviting.

"This is going to be interesting," he said. "These make-out train berths are damned narrow."

She looked down at the berth. "It's big enough if we're laying one upon the other."

"Yeah, you're right," he said, a little embarrassed by how quickly his manhood had hardened and was standing up tall and eager.

"You're *really* big," she said, eyes dropping to his erection. "Jasper wasn't nearly so large. And often when he was drunk, he could hardly get it to stand up at all. His thing was more like a limp sausage."

" 'Limp sausage!' "

"That's what it reminded me of," Lucy said solemnly. "But what you have there reminds me of a giant pink salami."

Longarm couldn't help himself and began to laugh. He laughed until his sides hurt and Lucy was laughing right with him. It broke the tension between them and

31

they embraced. Longarm was careful not to press too hard on her split lip as he kissed the woman and then laid her down on the berth.

"I'm going to try and keep my weight mostly off you, Lucy."

"All right," she said, spreading her short, but shapely legs wide. "I'm ready for you, Custis. So come on in slow and easy."

Longarm kept all of his upper body weight on his arms and Lucy guided his manhood slowly into her tight honey pot. Longarm sighed with pleasure. "How does it feel so far?"

"Huge, but nice," she assured him. "Move it slow and let's see how it feels as you go deeper."

Longarm was very careful as he slipped deeper into Lucy half expecting a cry or maybe even the feel of something different inside of her womb. But Lucy didn't feel any different inside than all the other women that he had made love to over the years. She was just smaller than most. He studied her face to make sure that there were no signs of pain and he saw only a contented smile. Lucy's eyes were shut tightly and now she was moving her hands down his sides and pressing down on his hips.

"Still good?" he asked, not yet convinced this was the right thing to do given the circumstances.

"Good and gettin' better by the moment," she said, her voice throaty with rising passion. "Come on, Custis, give it all to me!"

Longarm was more than happy to oblige. He sank his throbbing shaft in, giving Lucy his full measure and she moaned with pleasure. "Hold still for a few moments," she begged. "Just stay in real deep like that and don't move a muscle."

"All right."

But it was hard for Longarm because he could feel his shaft humming with intensity and wanting to piston in and out of this woman. Yet, he didn't dare get too energetic for fear of injuring the baby she was forming way up inside.

"All right," she whispered, her face warm on his chest. "Go on now. Do it like you would with any woman you care about very much."

He gulped and stammered. "When I go I won't *drown* the baby or anything, will I?"

"Of course not!" she said, giggling. "Now forget about that and make beautiful love to me."

Longarm needed no urging. He began to move his manhood inside of Lucy around and around in an ellipsis as Lucy lifted her hips and thighs higher and held him tight.

"Any pain?" he asked, giving her one last chance to stop this sweet madness.

"No, only pleasure."

Then Lucy began to get very excited and she started thrusting her hips upward. It was all that Longarm needed to tell him that it was fine to have his fill of this woman.

And so as the train rocked along somewhere north of Colorado Springs, Longarm and Lucy made good love. They took their time and made it last for miles and miles and both were grinning from ear to ear. Finally, when Lucy could stand it no longer, she pulled him down tight on her body and clutched the backs of his legs with both heels.

"Come on, Darling!" she pleaded. "Give it to me now. Give it to me, please!"

Longarm forgot everything except the feel of Lucy

under his body and the heat that was making them both so slippery that their bellies gave off loud sucking sounds.

When Longarm finally exploded inside of the woman, he was half mad with passion and Lucy was crying out in ecstasy as her body shuddered and jerked upward straining with surprising joy and power.

Chapter 5

The trip to Flagstaff was long, but definitely enjoyable for both Longarm and Lucy. They had made love often and so it was almost disappointing when they climbed off the train and made their way into the little railroad and mining town high in the mountains of northern Arizona.

"Where exactly is it that your sister lives?" Longarm asked as they checked into adjoining rooms at the Pinetop Hotel.

"She lives in a little settlement named Sedona. Claire said it was surrounded by pretty rocks and had a nice stream running through it where you can catch trout."

"I've heard of Sedona. It's supposed to be quite scenic," Longarm told her. "You rest in your hotel room while I find out if there's a stagecoach service that will take us there."

She looked at him with surprise and delight. "Are you really going with me?"

"Sure! You didn't think that I was just going to dump you off here in Flagstaff, did you?"

"I didn't know what your plans were."

"I am in a hurry to get down to the San Carlos Reservation, but Sedona isn't much out of my way. And besides, how long has it been since you've heard from your sister?"

Lucy thought about that for a moment. "A couple of years. Jasper didn't like me to stay in contact with Claire."

"Why not?"

Lucy shrugged. "He just didn't like me being close to anyone except himself."

"Your late husband was a twisted and possessive man," Longarm told her. "I just hope that your sister in Sedona isn't upset at you for breaking off contact."

"Me, too. If she doesn't take me in, where can I go?"

"Well, you sure wouldn't like it in Canyon City," Longarm replied. "Boomtowns are the worst place imaginable for a young woman."

"I'm sure that Claire will take me," Lucy said. "She and I were always close as sisters and she has a good and understanding husband."

"In that case," Longarm told her, "you have nothing to fret about. I'm going to find out how we can get to Sedona. I'll be back before too long. You should rest easy."

"I will," Lucy promised. "But I have to tell you that I was wishing that our train ride would never end."

Longarm had to grin because he had felt exactly the same way.

As luck would have it there was a stagecoach company that ran daily to Sedona so Longarm bought two tickets.

"We leave at eight o'clock sharp," the stagecoach

36

owner informed him. "So don't be late or you'll have to stay over here in Flagstaff an extra day."

"We'll be there on time," Longarm promised. "And do you know if there's a stagecoach that runs from Sedona to the San Carlos Apache Reservation?"

"There ain't one." The stagecoach owner studied Longarm for a minute. "You don't look like an Indian agent and you don't look like a miner. What would you want to go there for?"

"I've got my reasons."

"Well," the man said, "it's none of my business, but I should tell you that there's a lot of trouble goin' on down in that country between the miners and the Apache. Canyon City is a powder keg ready to explode. From what I've heard, they are about to have a war break out over water. Gonna be a lot of blood spilled and probably some scalps taken, I reckon."

"That's what I've heard, too," Longarm replied, putting his tickets in his vest pocket. "See you at eight o'clock tomorrow morning."

"I've got a full coach," the man said. "Trip takes about five hours. You'll like the views as we go down through Oak Creek Canyon. But as for gettin' to San Carlos and Canyon City, you'll either have to walk or buy a horse. And I do happen to know a good horse trader in Sedona that will treat you fairly."

"That will help," Longarm told the man. "How far is it from Sedona to Canyon City?"

"I dunno. Never been down there and don't want to go. But, if I had to guess, I'd say it would take a man at least a couple of days of hard riding to get to Canyon City. The country over there is rugged."

Longarm appreciated this information and so he

thanked the stagecoach owner and headed back to the hotel. After buying both train and stagecoach tickets for Lucy Dooley he figured he was already getting low on funds. Maybe he'd better wire Billy Vail giving a brief report, but not mentioning Lucy. He'd also ask that additional travel money be sent to Sedona. Otherwise, it was sure going to be lean times on the trail south.

The next day proved to be one of the nicest of the trip. As promised, the ride down to Sedona was spectacular with Oak Creek gushing down through the red-rocked canyon on its way south. Sedona itself was breathtaking with its magnificent red rocks. When Longarm and Lucy arrived in the little settlement they immediately asked if anyone knew where Lucy's sister lived.

"Her last name is Walker," Lucy told the old man who was sitting under an oak tree smoking his corncob pipe. "Mrs. Claire Walker." Beside him was a yellow dog whose head was resting on the old man's foot.

"Mrs. Walker lives just up the street, fourth house on the right. One with the white picket fence that's covered with red roses."

Lucy laughed. "That would be Claire's place, all right. She was always fond of roses."

The old man nodded. "She's a fine lady. You even look like your sister, ma'am."

"She's prettier."

"Not unless my eyes are playing tricks on me," the old man said before he got up and walked away with his yellow dog trailing along behind.

Lucy squared her shoulders and looked nervously up at Longarm. "I'm worried," she admitted. "What if . . ."

"It'll work out," Longarm interrupted. "I'm sure that Claire will greet you with open arms."

"But what will she say when I tell her that I'm pregnant?"

"I don't know," Longarm admitted. "But I'd wait awhile to tell her. Let your sister get used to seeing you around a bit and to get reacquainted. Then tell her."

"I'm not sure that I can lie to her about Jasper."

"Then don't," Longarm advised. "But give it a little time."

Lucy nodded in agreement. "All right. Let's go."

When they came to the house with the picket fence and roses, Longarm took Lucy's hand and escorted her through the gate and up to the front door. They knocked and a moment later Claire was standing in front of them. Longarm was amazed by the physical resemblance between the two sisters. They were almost identical twins although Claire was a little older and taller.

For a moment, the sisters stared speechless at each other and then Claire flung open the door wide and hugged Lucy, squealing with joy. "My goodness, Lucy, what a wonderful surprise to see you again!"

Custis just stood back at the edge of the porch and said nothing. He was enjoying himself and discovered that he was as relieved as Lucy was that this reunion was so joyous.

"And this tall, handsome man must be Mr. Jasper Dooley," Claire said after a few minutes of hugging.

"No," Lucy said, "this is Marshal Custis Long from Denver. Mr. Long was good enough to escort me down here to visit you."

"I'm pleased to meet you, Marshal."

"Thank you, ma'am. Lucy has told me all about you so the pleasure is mine."

"You are very kind." Claire looked around. "Lucy, where is your husband?"

Lucy collected herself and took a deep breath. "The truth is, Claire, that my husband is dead. He died on the train."

Claire's eyes widened with confusion. "Died on the train coming down here to visit me?"

Lucy's lower lip quivered but she held her composure. "That's right. Jasper died on the train."

"But Jasper *was* a young man, wasn't he?"

"Yes," Lucy admitted. "But Jasper was . . . well, sort of on the wild side and he had a very bad temper. That's how come my husband was shot to death in a gunfight."

Claire's hand flew to her mouth. "Oh, dear heavens! How terrible!"

"It wasn't pretty," Lucy agreed. "It was bad."

Claire turned to Custis. "Marshal, were you present when this tragedy happened?"

Longarm shifted his feet in discomfort. "Actually, Mrs. Walker, I was."

"Was the man who shot my sister's husband arrested for his murder?"

"I'm afraid that *I* was the one that killed Lucy's late husband. He was drunk and crazy when he got on the train. He meant to harm your sister and there was no choice but to punch his permanent ticket."

Claire shook her head in amazement. "I have a feeling that you've both left a lot unsaid. Come inside and tell me all about it. Lucy, no wonder you look so pale and peaky. I'll make you and Marshal Long glasses of cold lemonade."

"That would be nice," Lucy said as her sister ushered them inside and then hurried into her kitchen.

Lucy sat down in a chair and whispered. "So much for my husband's heroic death story, huh?"

Longarm just shrugged. "Once you get caught up in a lie, it generally leads to a whole bunch more lies. Telling your sister the truth straight out is probably the best way to handle this. But I still would wait on telling her that you are with child."

Lucy was about to say something back when Claire rushed into the parlor with two glasses of lemonade. "Here you both go." The woman sat down in a chair. "Now, Lucy, you must tell me all about what happened to Jasper and how you are holding up to the strain."

While Lucy related the sad story of her late, drunken husband, Longarm sat back and let his mind wander as he looked around the parlor at the furnishings and the shelf of books. He could see that Claire and her husband had done well for themselves here in Sedona. The house was large and comfortable while the household furniture was impressive and expensive. Along the south wall was a floor to ceiling bookshelf and it was heavily laden with tomes. Most of the Walker books were classics, but Longarm also saw the latest and most popular works. Among them was *Ben-Hur* by author Lew Wallace, a highly successful historical romance about the early Christians in the Roman Empire, which Longarm had read and greatly enjoyed. He also spotted *A Tramp Abroad* by Mark Twain. The popular work was a delightful travel narrative based on a walking tour of Germany, Switzerland and Italy. Like most of Twain's writing this work was filled with humor and it had actually made Longarm want to visit Europe.

When Lucy was finished telling her sister about the death of her husband she began to weep. Longarm turned his attention away from the books and started to go to Lucy's side, but Claire beat him to it as she knelt and held her sister while saying to Longarm, "Despite Mr. Dooley's temper, Lucy must have loved her husband very much. She's taking this hard."

"Yes, she is," Longarm agreed. He was about to say more but Lucy suddenly blurted, "Oh, Claire, that's only half of my sorrow! You see, I'm *pregnant*!"

Longarm groaned, worried that sympathy would now turn to contempt or shock. He was wrong, however, because Claire let out a cry and hugged her sister even more tightly. "When is your baby due?"

"I don't know."

"Why are you sure that you're with child? You don't show it."

"I'm sure that I'm perhaps a month along. Maybe two."

"What a sad thing that your husband won't ever get to see his child!" Claire exclaimed. "But I'm so happy for you!"

Lucy stammered, "You are?"

"Of course! My husband and I have been trying to have a baby for years, but have not been so blessed. And to think that now we'll have one in this very house. Oh, dear heaven what a joy!"

Longarm wanted to crush the woman with gratitude. Instead, he just smiled and drank some more lemonade. It was obvious that Lucy had done the right thing and that her sister was a saint.

Longarm just hoped that Mr. Walker also possessed such a generous and forgiving nature.

After an hour or more of listening to the sisters catch up on their childhoods and more recent histories, Longarm excused himself and headed back to the hotel. Maybe, since Claire had insisted that her sister move in immediately, he could get a refund on the room that he'd rented for Lucy. The main thing was that Lucy was in good and loving hands and that she and her baby would be well taken care of. Longarm resolved that when he finished the San Carlos business, he would pass back through Sedona just to see how Lucy was getting along.

Tomorrow he would buy a horse . . . providing that authorization for additional travel money was waiting in the telegraph operator's office. And then, he would strike out for Canyon City and try to put a stop to a whole lot of bloodshed.

Chapter 6

"Are you *sure* that there's no money waiting here for me?" Longarm asked the telegraph operator with an edge to his voice.

"Yes, sir! I mean, no, sir. No money."

"Damn," Longarm swore in exasperation. He paced around the room for a moment, then said, "I'll be back later today, just in case the money was wired. After that, I have to leave town and I'll need that travel money sent on to the telegraph office in Canyon City."

"There isn't any telegraph office in Canyon City," the man explained. "Sorry."

"Then where is there a telegraph office down in that part of Arizona?"

The operator shrugged and adjusted the spectacles on his beaked nose. "I have no earthly idea, Marshal. But, if you leave me the postage, I'll forward money down to Fort Carlos. There's a small, but legitimate United States army post there and I'm sure that they would hold any funds you are receiving right there for you. After all, you're all working for the same government. Right?"

"Right," Longarm snapped. "I'll be back later."

He had gotten the name of a supposedly "honest" horse trader from the stagecoach owner. The Sedona horse trader's name was Wild Horse Willy. No last name. "Wild Horse Willy is a good man. None better when it comes to judging horseflesh. And you tell him that Chuck Beasley referred you to him. Wild Horse is a friend of mine and he'll take care of you right."

"I'm sure he will," Longarm had replied, not believing a single word of that story.

Now, Longarm was in sort of tight financial fix. As he approached the stables owned by Wild Horse Willy he removed his wallet and counted his money twice. He had a miserly twenty-two dollars. Hell, Longarm thought, that wasn't even enough to buy the food and supplies he'd need to get to Canyon City.

But twenty-two dollars was what he had and that meant he had no choice but to hock or sell something. Fortunately, he did possess a nice 14-karat gold ring and a fine silver money clip that, together, were worth at least fifty dollars of any man's money. If he could scrape together a total of seventy-five dollars, Longarm figured that he could rent a horse and saddle and outfit himself properly with a used but serviceable Winchester repeating rifle for the trip to San Carlos. If he was real fortunate, the money he'd requested from Denver would arrive soon and he'd be back in the chips. Billy Vail was not a cheapskate and he'd send at least another fifty dollars.

"I'll send him another telegram before I leave Sedona," Longarm told himself as he marched into the stables in search of a good, but cheap horse and saddle to rent.

"Yes, sir! Can I help you this fine day?"

Longarm turned to see a man that could be none

other than Wild Horse Willy. Willy stood about six-foot-six and had shoulders as wide as a door and a thick, but filthy beard that appeared to contain the partial contents of his last dozen meals.

"Chuck Beasley sent me to see you about a horse."

"Who?"

"Mr. Chuck Beasley ... the guy who owns the stagecoach line that runs from Flagstaff down here and back."

"Oh, him. Sure. Good old Chucky."

Longarm said, "Chuck said you'd treat me right with a good rent horse at a good price. And to tell you the truth I'm a little low on funds."

"What a shame," the giant said without a hint of sympathy. "I guess Chucky didn't tell you that I don't rent horses to strangers. I've had some of them rent a horse from me and then just keep on riding."

"I'm a federal officer of the law."

"Even worse than a thievin' stranger," Wild Horse Willy mused, tugging at his crusty beard. "A lawman is likely to get shot or ambushed. And do you think that whoever drills him is going to bring back my horse as a token of his good will?"

Longarm was getting exasperated. "Look," he said, "there is a lot of trouble brewing down in Canyon City between the miners and the San Carlos Apache. I've been sent here all the way from Denver to try to defuse the situation. Now what can you do for me?"

Wild Horse Willy pulled out a snot rag, honked loudly a few times and eyed Longarm with a cold and calculating eye. "How much money do you have to buy one of my fine horses?"

"I've got about twenty dollars in cash."

"Hell! Twenty dollars!" The huge man began to laugh with mirth. "I wouldn't loan you my *yard goat* for a lousy twenty dollars!"

"And," Longarm said, deciding that he hated this big, coarse man, "I've got a fine gold ring and a silver money clip worth at least seventy-five dollars."

Wild Horse stopped laughing. "Let's see 'em."

Longarm got his money clip out and showed the stable owner his handsome gold ring.

"Hmmm, take the ring off your finger."

Longarm did as asked, wondering why.

Wild Horse Willy took the ring in his huge, filthy hand, studied it closely for a moment and then *bit* it!

"What the hell are you doing!" Longarm shouted, grabbing the man's thick wrist and tearing his ring free. "Are you crazy?"

But Wild Horse Willy wasn't listening. "Any of my tooth marks on 'er?" he asked.

Longarm inspected his ring. "No."

"Means there ain't that much gold in that ring. Let's see that money clip."

"Not if you're going to bite it."

"I won't."

Longarm removed his money and handed the money clip to the giant. "It's top-grade silver."

"Hmmm," Wild Horse Willy mused, finger to his lips. "Marshal, I'll give you twenty dollars for the ring and ten for the money clip in trade on a *good* horse."

"And saddle, halter, bridle and blanket."

"No, Mr. Lawman, I sure couldn't do that," Wild Horse Willy said. "Not for a *part* gold ring that I couldn't wear and a money clip with no money in it."

Longarm had about had it with this hulking idiot. "Are there any other stables or horse traders in Sedona?"

Wild Horse Willy folded his powerful arms across his barrel chest. "Nope."

"Dammit, then what can you give me for the ring and the money clip?"

"Them and your twenty dollars cash will get you what you need to reach Canyon City, providing you take it slow."

"I'm in a hurry!"

"Hmmm. Tell you what I'll do, Marshal." Wild Horse Willy's eyes widened as if he'd just come up with a wonderful idea. "I'll take your money, ring and money clip in trade for a Missouri mule."

"Hell, no!" Longarm hadn't even needed to think about it.

Wild Horse Willy shrugged his shoulders. "In that case, we ain't goin' to do business, Mr. Lawman. And I got better things to do than to waste my time with a man without hardly any money and a ring with only a little gold in it."

He started to leave but Longarm said, "Wait a minute. Haven't you got an ugly young horse with speed that nobody wants?"

"Nope. Just the ugly Missouri mule, but he's sinful strong. Did you know that mules are a lot more sure-footed than horses?"

"Is that a fact?"

"Yes, it is," Wild Horse Willy said solemnly. "And this particular mule is a goodun'."

"All right. Show me your ugly Missouri mule."

The stable owner led Longarm around a barn to a little corral where the ugliest black mule Longarm had ever seen stood staring at them with interest. Not only was the beast incredibly ugly, he was immense. Like a draft horse.

"You're right about one thing, Wild Horse. That mule is really big and ugly."

"Best kind of mule to have. No one will want to steal him from you, Marshal."

"I can believe that. Is he well broke?"

"Yep! He is broke to pull a wagon or to saddle and ride."

Longarm studied the mule with more than a little trepidation. "I dunno," he hedged. "I had it in my mind to rent a horse and what you're showing me is a far cry from that, I tell you."

"A man has to do what a man has to do," Willy said, stroking his beard as if he were Moses laying down some great wisdom from the mountain.

"Show me the saddle that would fit him," Longarm said, realizing he had very little bargaining power.

Fifteen minutes later, the mule was saddled and Longarm was standing at its side. "Does this animal have a name?" Longarm asked.

"I call him Ugly."

"Good name." Longarm had never been reduced to riding a mule before. "How about you mounting up first and then riding Ugly around this corral a few times before I try him?"

"I'm too big and I have a bad back." To emphasize his point, Wild Horse put a hand in the small of his back and made a face. "Marshal, if you want to buy Ugly, you need to ride him right here in this corral and get acquainted."

"I don't want to get acquainted with Ugly," Longarm said. "But it looks as if I have no choice."

"Correct."

Longarm made sure that Ugly's cinch was tight before he jammed his foot in the stirrup and swung on board. Sitting in the rotting saddle and looking forward was a whole new view for Longarm. "Holy cow! Ugly's ears are so big it's like peeking through a couple of tree stumps! And his head is as big as a woman's hope chest."

Wild Horse ignored the unflattering remarks concerning his mule. "He's a goer, though. We got a deal, Marshal?"

Longarm gave Ugly a nudge with his heels and the Missouri mule walked out and when reined he went the right general direction.

"Reins real good, don't he?" Willy hooked his thumbs in his suspenders and spit a long stream of yellow tobacco juice at the ground. "Do you know a damn thing about mules, Mister Lawman?"

"Only that they're stubborn and ugly."

"They're also geniuses compared to horses," Willy said. "Ugly is twice as smart as my dog and even smarter than my sow. He won't step into a boggy place and, if he should step into a hornet's nest, he won't go crazy like a horse and start buckin' and runnin'. Same thing if he steps into a wad of barbed wire. Mules won't spook and take you over the edge of a cliff, either. Why, I've known a lot of men that wouldn't ride nothin' but a mule."

"Save it for your next sale."

"And," Willy continued, "when you ride into a town on Ugly, everyone will take notice."

"I don't want people to take notice of me."

"Yeah, I guess I can understand that."

"So have we got a deal?"

"I guess."

"Then hand over that ring, money clip, and your twenty dollars."

51

"Only the ring and money clip and *ten* dollars," Longarm said. "That's the best I can do because I have to have some money to feed myself and this mule on the ride over to Canyon City."

"Mr. Lawman, you sure do drive a hard bargain."

"Bullshit!"

Longarm dismounted from the towering Ugly and gave the big man back the ring and money clip along with about half his remaining cash. Just then, Ugly's massive head swung around and the mule bit Longarm in the back!

"Owww!" Longarm howled, jumping away as his hand flashed to the butt of his six-gun.

"Don't you dare shoot that mule!"

"Well the son of a bitch just took a bite out of me!"

"Yeah. I guess you didn't know that until you get well acquainted you can't turn your back on a Missouri mule. And the other thing is that they need to like you."

"*Like* me?" Longarm shouted, rubbing his painful back and wondering if it was bleeding. "What kind of nonsense is that?"

"Ain't nonsense," Willy said, counting the cash. "I told you that these mules are the geniuses of the animal world. If they get their feelings hurt or feel that they are being mistreated or ignored . . . they don't like it."

"I don't want an animal that I can't turn my back on. What other bad habits has Ugly got?"

"None that I know of."

Longarm cussed under his breath, then hung his head in defeat and despair. "All right. I'll take Ugly, but only because I have no choice."

"You'll come to love him," Willy promised, suddenly breaking into a wide and toothless grin. "And when you get to the San Carlos Reservation those Apache will start to drool cause they favor mule above all other kinds of red meat."

"Good," Longarm said. "Then I can sell him to them at a modest profit and buy a *real* mount."

Willy was trying to cram the gold ring onto his pinkie finger, but failed so he stuck it in his pocket along with the cash.

"I got work to do now, Mr. Lawman. Our business is finished and I wish you good luck. Just remember what I told you about mules and you'll do fine with Ugly. To be honest, I kinda hate to see him go. People liked to come around just to watch him try to stomp my chickens and dog. He'd pretend that he was dozin' off and then he'd go after them in a rush. It was a great show."

Longarm groaned. He had a feeling he had just make a terrible mistake and that he might never even survive to reach Canyon City.

"Where is the best place in this town to buy some supplies?"

"I got a friend named Jesse who owns a general store just up the street. Tell him that I sent you and he'll give you a real good deal."

"Sure," Longarm said with unconcealed sarcasm, "just like Chucky's recommendation made you decide to give me such a good deal on this Missouri mule."

"That's right, Mr. Lawman." Wild Horse Willy chuckled as he turned and walked away.

Chapter 7

Longarm was half ashamed to ride through Sedona on Ugly, but there was little choice. He stopped at the telegraph operator's office where he was greatly relieved to find that Billy Vail had wired him additional travel funds along with a terse message to "Quit messing around and get to Canyon City at once!"

Longarm didn't mind the terse order from his boss because he was so happy to get some money. He now regretted trading off his gold watch and money clip toward the ugly black mule, but that was finished. He had a mount and he would make the best of it until he reached the San Carlos Indian Reservation. And so, despite some funny looks from the people on the street, Longarm tied the mule to a hitching post and went into the general store where he bought supplies. He preferred to travel light so he bought a minimum amount of food for himself along with some grain for the Missouri mule.

"That your ugly black mule tied out front?" Jesse asked, staring at the huge animal.

"Just borrowing him," Longarm mumbled.

The store owner snorted, "It's a cryin' shame that someone hasn't put that ugly beast out of its misery."

"Ring up my bill," Longarm ordered, out of patience with the people he'd had to deal with in Sedona. "And tell me where I can buy a good used Winchester repeating rifle."

"There's a gunsmith just two doors up the street. He'll sell you whatever you need. Tell him that Jesse sent you and he'll probably give you a better deal."

"Sure, like you just have given me a break because I was referred here by Wild Horse Willy."

Jesse blinked not understanding. Longarm picked up his supplies and went out to tie them down behind his saddle. Ugly laid back his great ears flat against his head and displayed his yellow teeth, but Longarm drew his six-gun and hissed, "Mule, if you bite me again I'll shoot you right here on the street and walk away while you're still bleeding and twitching."

Longarm and Ugly looked deeply into each others' eyes. Then Ugly seemed to decide that he had met his match and his ears turned forward.

"Good damned decision," Longarm told the mule as he went to visit the gunsmith's shop.

"Jesse sent me over here and said that you'd give me a good deal on a used rifle."

"Jesse said that?" the man sitting at a bench working on an old shotgun asked with obvious surprise.

"That's right," Longarm replied.

"Hell, I can't stand Jesse and he can't stand me," the man confessed. "If you're a friend of Jesse's then I might have to charge you *extra*."

"I'm no friend of his."

"What exactly you need today?"

"A Winchester repeater. I'd prefer a Model '73 in

good working condition and accurate. Also a box of cartridges."

"I think I have what you need, mister."

The rifle's stock was scarred, but the action worked smoothly. "Have you fired this rifle and is it accurate?"

"I test fire everything before I sell it," the gunsmith said. "I had to do a little work on this one, but I guarantee it is in perfect working order now. If you don't trust me you can take it out in the alley and test fire the weapon."

"That won't be necessary. How much?"

"Fifteen dollars and that is a bargain."

Longarm agreed and he spent another three dollars on cartridges. Satisfied, he started to walk out the door when gunsmith said, "How come you wear your Colt Model T butt forward?"

Longarm shrugged. "I reckon it's because I like it that way."

"Are you quick with it out of the holster?"

"Quick enough." Longarm figured that the gunsmith wanted him to demonstrate, but he wasn't going to give him the satisfaction.

"You look like a serious man," the gunsmith said, "but I never thought wearing a gun backward for a cross-draw made any sense."

"Not to you, maybe, but this works for me," Longarm told the man as he closed the door.

Longarm would have liked to buy a rifle scabbard for the Winchester, but didn't want to spend the extra cash so he just tied the rifle to the saddle and mounted the tall mule.

"Which way to the San Carlos Indian Reservation?" he asked a man standing on the boardwalk watching him with interest.

The man gave Longarm a look that left little doubt that he thought the tall stranger must be awfully stupid.

"Stranger, just take the road just south of here across the river and then head southeast along the old Beckman Road. You'll meet wagons and travelers all along the way who will keep you from getting lost. Lots of people going to Canyon City these days to prospect for gold. You a prospector?"

"Nope."

"I didn't think so."

"Thanks for the directions."

"You're welcome. Shame you got to ride such an ugly mule. He looks to be about as friendly as a teased rattlesnake."

"I didn't buy him to impress anyone or to make a friend," Longarm told the man as he reined the mule around and headed south.

Just before he reined Ugly south he heard the man on the boardwalk mutter, "That fella is just a dumb ass riding an ugly mule. He'll probably get lost along the way or that black mule will kick him in the head and kill him."

Longarm didn't pay the man any attention. He was heading to Canyon City and the San Carlos Reservation and by damned he'd get there one way or the other and he'd take care of business.

"Custis!"

It was Lucy who had seen him passing by on Ugly and who wanted to tell him good-bye.

Longarm reined the mule around then rode back to the girl.

"How are you doin', Lucy?"

"I'm fine, thank you. But were you just going to leave without even saying good-bye to me?"

The question caught him by surprise. "Well," he stammered, "I . . ."

Lucy came up closer but stopped when Ugly laid back his ears in warning.

"Best stay back from this Missouri mule," Longarm cautioned. "He's not to be trusted."

She frowned at the animal. "Then why didn't you buy a good horse instead of that awful beast?"

Longarm didn't want to tell Lucy that she'd cost him so much extra money that he had nearly gone broke and had to trade off his ring and money clip. "Well, I guess I must have had a moment of temporary insanity."

But Lucy shook her head as she realized the truth. "No, you didn't, Custis. You spent your money helping me to get here and so that mule was the only thing that you could afford."

"Seeing you reunited with your sister and brother-in-law and knowing that you and your baby will be loved and cared for made it all worth while," Longarm said, cocking back his hat and noticing that people were staring.

"I won't let you leave until you promise to come back when you're finished in Canyon City."

"I promise. Now I'd better ride along."

"Custis, I have one question to ask before you go."

"Keep your voice down," he said, "because people around here have big ears."

Lucy lowered her voice. "If everything works out for you, would you consider . . ."

"What?" he asked.

"Well, maybe coming back to stay?"

Longarm smiled. "I'll come back, but not to stay," he said. "I'm not ready to settle down in one place even though I have to admit this town is pretty and you're even prettier."

Lucy blushed.

"But the thing is, Lucy, I'm your past and you need to be looking to the future. There are a lot of young men around here that will come calling on you before long. Just use your head as well as your heart. If you do that you and your baby will be fine."

"Okay."

There were tears in Lucy's eyes when Longarm tipped his hat to her and reined Ugly around and headed for Canyon City.

Longarm was beginning to fear that if he didn't stop getting sidetracked, the Apache and the miners would kill each other all off.

Chapter 8

The trip over to Canyon City was a difficult climb up onto the Mogollon Rim into some of the most spectacular, but wildest country Longarm had ever traveled. His black Missouri mule proved to be an excellent trail mount with sure feet and good instincts. In fact, the harder the climb and the tougher the terrain the more Ugly seemed ready for the challenge.

On his second day out Longarm spotted a body lying facedown in the bottom of a ravine. He would never even have seen the man had it not been for Ugly acting up and refusing to continue along the trail. The mule's big ears were pointing down into the steep ravine like a bird dog on the hunt and the animal was snorting as if he'd seen a ghost.

"I'd better hike down there and see if that man is alive or dead," Longarm said, tying the mule to a pine and then taking his rifle just in case there were ambushers or highwaymen lurking about in the vicinity.

It was a steep climb down into a ravine and when Longarm reached the body, he grabbed one of the boots and pulled the man out of the brush. His first impression was that the man was dead because there was dried blood on his shirt and even more matted in his mop of silver hair. But when Longarm rolled the man over onto his back he saw a fluttering of eyelids.

Longarm cupped his hands in the little nearby stream and splashed water over the man who looked to be in his seventies. "Mister, can you hear me?"

Suddenly the old man's rough hand reached for his holster, but his gun was missing. He next tried to draw his Bowie knife from its leather sheath, but that was missing as well.

"Easy," Longarm said. "Old-timer, I'm afraid you've been defanged. Whoever shot you took your gun and knife and probably a lot more."

The man's eyes were dull with pain and probably blurred because he kept blinking rapidly. His lips were swollen and that indicated to Longarm that the man had been physically beaten before being thrown off the trail above and left to die in this deep ravine.

When the man began to thrash and fight Longarm said, "Take it easy! I'm here to *help* . . . not hurt you. Where are you shot?"

The old man grew still and his chest began to heave as he tried to breathe. But there was a faint rattling sound in his chest that was ominous so Longarm said, "Just rest easy. You've obviously gotten a real back crack on the skull. As for the other, well, I'll find the bullet hole quick enough. If we're lucky, it passed through you. If not, I'll have to dig it out. Either way, you've lost a lot of blood and need to be still."

Longarm saw the man's lips move as he tried, but failed, to speak. He opened the man's shirt and saw where a bullet had ricocheted off a rib and come to rest just under the left arm. "Old-timer, you're lucky that the slug didn't deflect into your lungs or heart. If it had done either, you'd already be knocking at heaven's door. I can see the lump of lead under your skin and I'll have it out in a moment or two, but you have to hold very still."

Longarm didn't know if the wounded man understood him or not, but he must have because he didn't jerk or thrash about anymore as Longarm used his knife to cut the skin and then dig out the misshapen lead slug. This caused a good deal of fresh bleeding, but not so much that it couldn't be contained by a tight bandage.

"Water!" the old man croaked.

Longarm glanced up at the trail above just in time to see someone rush to Ugly's side and try to steal the big mule. But Ugly hee-hawed and kicked the thief so hard that the man came tumbling over the edge of the ravine and rolled down to the creek. The would-be mule thief was dressed in ragged pants and shirt with a small knapsack tied to his back.

"Hold on just a minute," Longarm said when he reached the young thief who was groaning in pain. Longarm drew his gun and pistol-whipped the man just hard enough to silence his groans and to make sure that he didn't attempt an escape. The young man sighed and lost consciousness.

"If there is one thing I hate it is a horse thief. Or, I guess in this case, a mule thief. I'll tend to him later."

Longarm hurried back to the older man and finished the bandaging job. He helped his patient into a sitting position and said, "We have to get you up to the trail and then I'll see that you get to a town. If Ugly will allow it, you can ride him and I'll lead him."

The old man's eyes fluttered open and he stared at Longarm then grunted, "Water, dammit!"

"All right!" Longarm eased the man over to the little creek and shoved his white whiskered face into the water. "If you don't want to wait to get to my canteen, then drink your fill of this muddy water."

The man did drink so much that Longarm thought he might burst. But when his thirst was finally satisfied he turned to Longarm and asked, "What's your name?"

"Custis Long. Did that young thief lying on the rocks over there do this to you?"

The old man stared at the unconscious highwayman. "No. The ones that jumped me were two other fellas. I never seen 'em until it was too late to defend myself. I remember them robbin' me and I tried to fight, but I didn't have a chance." The old man sadly patted his shirt and pants pockets. "They took every last cent I had in the world."

"Maybe we'll find them in Canyon City," Longarm said, wanting to give the man some reason for hope. "If we do, then we'll get your money and mule back. But the main thing is that you're still alive and you're going to pull through this once we get you up to the trail and on my black mule."

The old man studied the long, steep slope. "I'm not sure that I can do that, mister."

"You have no choice," Longarm told him. "Can you stand up if I give you a boost?"

"I'll try."

The old man got up, but he was real shaky. "After taking a few deep and steadying breaths he said, "My name is J.D. Gaston. People just call me Gassy because I fart so much."

To emphasize the point Gassy cut a windy that was one of the rankest Longarm had ever smelled.

"Whew! I see what they mean. Well, Gassy, we got to climb."

"I'll give it my best." Gassy looked over at the unconscious man lying on the rocks. "What happened to him?"

"He tried to steal my Missouri mule, but it must have kicked him right over the ledge and he rolled down here to join us. He was hurt pretty good, but I laid the barrel of my Colt across his skull just to make sure he'd cause us no more grief."

"Leave him," Gassy pronounced without a shred of pity. "It was a couple just like him that laid me low and took everything I owned in this world and left me to die down here in the brush."

"I think he'll recover," Longarm said, deciding that he didn't want to go to the bother of arresting the thief and therefore letting everyone in Canyon City know right away that he was a federal lawman. "And he can climb his way out when he wakes up a sadder, but wiser man."

Gassy's face twisted with anger. "If you lend me your pistol, I'll shoot him dead."

"No," Longarm said, pointing Gassy at the slope. "Let's just leave him to wake up in a world of pain."

Longarm had to admit that Gassy was a real gamer. For although he was quite old, in pain and possessed a pair of lungs that were far from being in the best of shape, the man doggedly attacked the steep and gravely slope. On the way up they had to stop three or four times, but they finally made it to the trail above where Gassy bent over and struggled desperately for breath.

"I should never have left the low desert country," the older man was finally able to gasp. "This high country just makes it harder than blazes for me to breathe."

"Then why did you leave the desert?"

"Too damned hot!" Gassy wheezed. "Why me and my mule both almost died down near Yuma this past summer. I figure I'm for certain goin' to hell when I breathe my last . . . which almost happened today . . . and I don't need to be already in a hell on Earth in a place like Yuma."

"Even so, you don't sound real good," Longarm said, checking his makeshift bandaging job to see if Gassy was bleeding again. Fortunately, he was not.

"What a hell of a handsome mule!" Gassy croaked, looking at Ugly for the first time. "By gawd, my mule Moses was a good-looker, but he couldn't hold a candle to the looks of your Missouri mule. How old is he?"

Longarm shrugged because he didn't care. "Damned if I know."

"I'll find out," Gassy said lurching toward Ugly to open his mouth and check his long yellow teeth.

"Don't do that!" Longarm cried in warning. "He bites!"

But Gassy had no fear of mules. And even though Ugly laid back his ears and showed his teeth, Gassy didn't seem to take notice. Instead he went right up to the mule, grabbed its massive lower jaw and pried his mouth open to study Ugly's teeth.

"He's only about five years old," Gassy pronounced. "Just a boy, really. And what a strong and good lookin' fella he is!"

"Mister, are you half blind?" Longarm asked in amazement. "Because you must be. That's the ugliest mule I've ever seen. Why everyone that sees him just stops and stares. Even his name is Ugly."

66

Gassy looked appalled. He appraised the black mule again and cried, "The hell you say!"

"The hell I *do* say."

Gassy laid his bloody head against the side of Ugly's jaw and petted the mule softly saying, "This big fella is one of the best lookin' mules I ever laid eyes upon. And you should be *ashamed* of yourself for thinkin' otherwise."

Longarm stood back and watched the old man stroke his black mule's head until Ugly closed his eyes with obvious contentment. "Gassy, I think now I've seen about everything. Why, that mule is pure mean and you've already got him acting like a pussycat."

Gassy grinned. "That's because I love mules and they always love me. You see they're so much smarter than horses and they know if a fella likes them and respects them or not. Now you can be sure that this mule knows that you think he's ugly and so he does not take real kindly to you. But, if you tell him he's a handsome devil and that you're proud to own such a fine animal as himself, then I promise you that his spirits and temperament will improve right away."

Longarm just listened to this and shook his head. "Well, to be honest," he said, "I have been impressed by that mule's strength, stamina and heart. Ugly goes right up a mountainside as if he was half goat and he never needs to stop and rest. And I told him once coming over here that I appreciated how much heart and wind he had."

"There you go," Gassy said, nodding his head in full agreement. "It's just like I was tellin' you. Mules are so smart they know if a man appreciates them or not. And you never want to mistreat a mule. Uh-uh! If you do, then they'll hate you forever and do their best to even the score."

"I'm not saying that I disagree with you, but I would still prefer a good saddle horse."

"Then you're a little bit the fool," Gassy said without batting an eye. "Where are you headed?"

"To Canyon City."

"So am I! Let's travel together."

Longarm thought that was a good idea because Gassy really didn't look fit enough to hike miles and miles through these tough mountains. So he drank from his canteen, tied his Winchester back on the saddle and said, "I'll help you get up in the saddle and I'll walk for awhile."

"Are you sure?" Gassy asked with genuine concern.

"Yep."

"You're a fine, fine man and it'll be a great pleasure to ride your mule a spell. I sure hope that the two men who ambushed me are in Canyon City so I can repay 'em the favor. Of course, I'll need to borrow your rifle and a pair of bullets."

"You just point those thieves out to me, old-timer, and I'll take care of the rest."

"Are you a gunman, a prospector or a gambler?"

Longarm considered the question only a moment before he replied, "I'm none of those things."

"Then what are you?"

"I'm an adventurer," Longarm said with a smile. "And a man who likes to stay on the move and to right wrongs."

"You don't look like Don Quixote to me!" Gassy laughed, cutting a fart that immediately set Ugly's ears to quivering.

Longarm started out walking. He really didn't

mind hoofing it awhile. And as they were leaving he thought he heard a faint cry from down in the ravine from the young thief who had been kicked by Ugly and then pistol-whipped by himself for good measure.

But Longarm didn't even bother to glance back down into the ravine. The young man could either climb out . . . or die . . . because to Longarm's uncomplicated way of thinking a man should reap exactly what he sowed.

Chapter 9

"There she be!" Gassy called when he and Ugly topped a ridge, "Canyon City! Come on up and see 'er!"

Longarm had walked every step of the way since he'd saved Gassy and he was exhausted and light-headed because they'd used up his food supplies a day earlier. "I'm trying!" he groused, giving it his all to top the final ridge.

"Well, what do you think?" Gassy asked. "Pretty good-sized little mining town, I reckon."

Longarm was out of breath and bent over for a few minutes, but then he straightened and gazed down on Canyon City. It was bigger than he'd expected. It boasted one main street with about a dozen buildings on each side and then a whole slew of shacks, corrals, barns and sheds randomly scattered all the way to the edges of a quarter-mile-wide canyon. Down one side of the canyon bubbled Canyon Creek where at least a hundred miners were hard at work prospecting for gold with pans, rockers and long toms.

"Looks like a swarm of ants down there," Gassy

observed. "Just like an ant hill that a boy stirred up with a stick."

"Yeah," Longarm said. "I'd guess there are almost a thousand people down there. I wonder how many of them are getting rich."

"Damn few," Gassy judged. "I've been to more boomtowns than I can remember and the only ones that get rich are those that don't dirty their hands. I'm talking about the businessmen that charge prices higher than an elephant's ass and the gamblers and whores and real estate shysters. Those bloodsuckers couldn't muster up enough grit to swing a pick or handle a shovel even if their worthless lives depended upon it."

Longarm didn't disagree and had nothing to add.

"I'll bet my mule is down there someplace," Gassy told him. "And when I find Moses, then I'll find the two sidewinders that stole him from me and I'll shoot 'em dead with your rifle."

"No, you won't," Longarm told the old man. "Because I'll handle it."

"You think I can't take care of my own troubles and settle my own scores?" Gassy demanded.

"I'm not saying that," Longarm told the old man. "I'm just saying that I should handle it."

"Why?"

Longarm saw no way around telling Gassy the truth. He reached into his vest pocket and showed the man his badge. "I'm a United States marshal sent here from Denver to try and sort out the troubles between the people of Canyon City and the San Carlos Apache."

"Well, I'll be danged!" Gassy cried. "I sure never figured you for a lawman."

"That's the way I like things," Longarm said. "There always comes a time when I have to show my badge and do my official duty, but I like to keep my business quiet until then."

"Meaning you'd like me not to say anything about you being a marshal?"

"Exactly."

"Then how are we supposed to settle up with the pair that stole my mule? And how am I supposed to get him back without a fight?"

"That's a good question," Longarm conceded. "And I don't have an answer right off the top of my head. But, if you'll point the pair out to me, I'll make sure that justice is served."

"And I'll get Moses back?" Gassy asked with skepticism.

"Yes, you'll get your mule back," Longarm promised.

"And what about my money, gun and other things those sidewinders took from me before they left me down in that ravine for dead."

"As much of it as they have left will be returned . . . and maybe even more," Longarm told the old man. "You have my word on it."

"That's good enough for me." Gassy cleared his throat. "But, Marshal, I'm as poor as a toothless coyote and skinnier than a bed slat. I got to have some money to buy a pan so that I can join them fellas down there in that stream. All the best claims will be taken and it might be a few days before I can pan enough gold to feed myself."

Longarm opened his wallet and gave Gassy five dollars. "Sorry I can't do better'n that, old-timer."

"It's all right," Gassy said, sticking out his hand. "I owe you my life and you've no apologizing to do on your part. And I'll help you down there in any way that I can. I mean that and you can count on me, Marshal."

"I may need a friend down there and I'll remember your offer." Longarm took up the reins on his black mule. "It would be better if we went down there separated. I expect you can understand."

"Sure I can." Gassy cut a long, slow one that caused Ugly's ears to twitch fast. "So long, Marshal."

"So long and when you spot those fellas that shot you and stole your mule, you look me up on the sly."

"I'll do 'er," Gassy promised.

Longarm mounted Ugly and headed down into the canyon. He was glad to be here at last and was hoping that the trouble he faced would not be any more difficult or dangerous than expected. But a man never knew what he was getting into until he jumped in with both feet.

"Say Marshal!"

Longarm reined up. "Yeah?"

"Those two that ambushed me. I think one of them called the other Diamondback."

"Diamondback?"

"Yeah. That's what one called the other."

"Damned strange name for a man," Longarm muttered as he rode down into the canyon. "Diamondback. Wonder how a man would get that kind of a handle."

Chapter 10

There were a lot of things that Longarm did not like
about boomtowns. They were usually lawless and at-
tracted the worst imaginable element of mankind. And
those few individuals who were honest, the simple
miners and laborers, were preyed upon by the rest of
the boomtown society. Longarm had seen a lot of
boomtowns in his years as a federal officer and most
of them didn't last even a year before the pay dirt
played out. When that happened the town was disman-
tled and carted off to another location where the gold
fever frenzy began anew.

As he rode Ugly down the single main street of
Canyon City, Longarm could feel the pulse beat of the
town and it was furious. No one arriving in this
overnight town had bothered to construct sidewalks so
the buildings just fronted the dirt street and many of
them had dirt floors. The air in Canyon City swarmed
with flies, dust and was punctuated by coarse laughter.
Longarm saw the usual prostitutes standing in front of
their cribs among the hawkers and gamblers . . . all
selling their souls for the almighty dollar.

A man of God who looked like the late Abraham

Lincoln stood on a stump with a tattered Bible in his bony hands and wore a frayed black frock coat as he shouted his message of repentance and eternal salvation. Not far from him a half dozen old Apaches sat under the shade of a cottonwood tree chewing tobacco, watching the people and sipping firewater. Longarm saw few children, no churches, and no cleanliness or courtesy offered or expected. In a town like Canyon City, it was every man and woman for theirselves. The only children he saw were a few Apache boys selling firewood and running errands for money.

Mainly there were saloons, hotels with false fronts, assay offices, real estate offices and gray canvas tents where a man could eat or sleep cheaply . . . and whorehouses. As he maneuvered his way through the bustling main street, Longarm witnessed two vicious brawls. In one, an older Apache was getting stomped mercilessly by a drunken miner. Longarm didn't want to set himself apart or reveal that he was a lawman, yet he simply couldn't let the beating continue so as he rode past the miner he casually clubbed him with the barrel of his Winchester knocking him out cold.

The old Apache looked up from the dirt through a haze of blood and gave Longarm a toothless and grateful smile as he and Ugly passed.

"Where can I board my mule?" Longarm called out to a miner unsteadily crossing the road.

The man studied Longarm's mule and shook his head. "He ain't worth boarding anywhere, mister. If I were you I'd take him down to the reservation and sell him for a couple dollars as dog or Apache meat. Better he gives you money than he takes your money. Damned ugliest mule I ever laid eyes upon."

"Where's a stable?" Longarm repeated, but this

time in a hard voice that shaved the smirk off the miner's face.

"Ride on down the road just a little ways and you'll see it on the left-hand side near the river. Potter's Stable. He'll sure get a laugh when he sees that unholy beast!"

Longarm easily found Potter's Stable. And damned if Potter didn't laugh, until Longarm told the man to shut up and take care of his ornery Missouri mule. Then Potter got serious and asked for more money than was fair. Longarm paid the man and made sure that Ugly was put up separate from any other animal and that he received a good measure of grain.

"Be careful around my mule," Longarm warned. "He is testy and he kicks and bites."

"If he kicks or bites me then I'll shoot him dead."

"Then I'd have to shoot *you* dead," Longarm said with a look that left no doubt that he meant his words. "Do you have any other mules being stabled here?"

"As a matter-of-fact I do have one," Potter told him. "Couple of fellas brought it in the day before yesterday. It's a lot better looking than this mule and he's for sale."

"I'd like to have a look at that mule."

"You a stinking mule skinner?"

"Nope. I just find mules . . . interesting," Longarm replied.

"The mule is around back. You won't be able to miss him. Price is thirty dollars and he's worth it. Fine animal, if you happen to like mules."

"I do and thanks."

Longarm walked around behind the stable and saw what had to be Gassy's mule Moses. He walked back to find Potter and said, "Where can I find the owner about buying that mule?"

"I have no idea where he's staying. He calls him-self Diamondback. Hell of a handle, isn't it?"

"That's for sure. What does he look like?"

"Oh, you'd spot him in a second even in a crowd. Big, big man. As tall as you and wider. He's about your age and has a diamondback rattlesnake tattooed on his cheek."

"Butt cheek?" Longarm asked without cracking a smile.

Potter's face colored with embarrassment. "Hell, no! The tattoo is on his *face*! You think he'd show off a butt tattoo?"

"I don't know," Longarm replied. "Any man strange enough to have his face tattooed might also have one on his butt."

"I don't want to talk about this anymore," Potter groused, looking extremely uncomfortable. "Dia-mondback and the other man who came in here with that mule are tough customers. I'd just as soon not have to deal with them anymore so I hope you buy that mule and then you take *both* mules the hell outta my stable. I never liked mules and I never liked mule skinners."

"Well," Longarm said, "not that it matters, but I don't think I like *you* very much either."

And with that, he shouldered his pack and Win-chester and walked straight into town.

Longarm stopped at the first of two board-built ho-tels in Canyon City. They weren't much too look at and the price of a tiny room was exorbitant, but he paid it not wishing to rent a cot by the hour in a damned tent. Then, he went to a saloon and bought a beer and turned to see Gassy standing at the other end of the room.

Gassy remembered not to acknowledge Longarm, but the old man could barely contain his obvious excitement. And when Gassy thought no one was looking, he pointed toward a back table where a big and very unhappy man was losing at cards.

Longarm took his beer and eased over in that general direction. Sure enough the man losing at the table was Diamondback and the man next to him was no doubt his partner.

Longarm watched the game with more than a casual interest. He could see that Diamondback was a reckless player who was steadily losing money and not taking it well. His partner was a smaller man with close-set eyes and thin lips. He was a far more skilled and conservative player who looked to Longarm to be a professional. Of the two of them who had robbed and left Gassy for dead while stealing his mule, Longarm decided that the smaller, heavily armed man might be the more dangerous.

Maybe, Longarm thought, this pair was running a crooked game together by sending signals between them and trying to look as if they were strangers. Having one of the partners lose some cash was a common distraction to the fact that the other partner was more than making up the pair's modest loses.

"Damn!" Diamondback shouted loud enough to attract the attention of everyone in the room. "I never had such bad luck in my life!"

Diamondback's partner shook his head sympathetically and raked in a fresh pile of money. "That's the way it goes sometimes, mister."

"Yeah, I guess so." Diamondback stared at his partner and snarled, "You wouldn't be cheatin' on me would you?"

"Hell, no!"

"You'd better not be or I'll send you to the Promised Land!"

Diamondback's partner stiffened with pretended anger. "Mister, you should be careful about how you shoot off your mouth."

For a moment every voice in the saloon fell silent. Then, Diamondback relaxed and threw in his cards with disgust. "I'm tapped out," he pronounced. "But, dammit, I'll come back and the next time my luck will be a whole lot better."

"Sure it will," Diamondback's partner said. "When a man's luck is running bad the best thing he can do is to quit and wait awhile until his luck changes to the good."

"You got that right." Diamondback grunted as he left the game.

The men sitting around the card table appeared relieved as Diamondback marched off to the bar and bellowed, "Bartender, gimme a double shot of whiskey! I lost twenty dollars over there at that table. I sure ain't happy about it, either."

Longarm decided that this was his chance to get Diamondback away from his partner where he'd be easier to handle so he went over to the big man and said in a friendly way, "Mister, I understand that you are boarding a mule over at Potter's Stable."

"So what business is that of yours?"

Longarm shrugged inoffensively. "I heard you'd like to sell that mule."

Diamondback turned and regarded Longarm eye to eye. No doubt he was wondering if this stranger knew that he'd left an old man dead on the trail and stolen the mule. "And just how'd you hear that?"

"I just boarded a mule of my own and the two of them might make a team," Longarm answered with a friendly smile. "So I was wondering how much money you want for that mule?"

"Thirty dollars," Diamondback said, relaxing.

"I might give you twenty."

Diamondback scoffed. "He's worth twenty-five of any man's money and I'll throw in a pack and halter."

Longarm considered this for a moment. "Is the mule sound and broke to the saddle?"

"Hell, yes. He's easier to ride than most horses."

Longarm pretended to consider this information carefully. Finally, he said, "I'd like to see *you* ride him before I pay twenty-five dollars."

It was clear that Diamondback wasn't in the mood to ride Moses, but equally clear that he would like to replenish the cash he'd just lost at the table. "Before I go out of my way to ride that mule, I need to see your money."

Longarm opened his wallet so that Diamondback could get a glimpse of his cash and know he had twenty-five dollars.

"All right," Diamondback said, as if he were making a huge concession. "I'll finish my beer and meet you over at Potter's Stable in about ten minutes."

"Sounds good," Longarm said, finishing his own beer and then leaving with Gassy about fifteen feet behind.

When Longarm stopped at a corner to light a cigar, Gassy eased up close and whispered, "He and that other smaller man are the ones that ambushed and left me for dead."

"I know. In a few minutes I'm going to meet Diamondback at Potter's and I'll arrest him. Then I'll come back here and do the same with his partner."

"What can I do to help?"

Longarm handled Gassy his Winchester. "If something goes wrong when I brace either one, shoot to kill."

"Be my pleasure!" And then perhaps because of his excitement Gassy cut a mean, snarling fart that sent Longarm hurrying off on his way.

Diamondback didn't show up for nearly a half hour. And when he did show up it was clear that he'd done more than just finish his *one* beer. His eyes were bloodshot and his manner was short.

"All right," Diamondback snapped. "Find me a damned saddle and bridle and I'll ride the mule. But you'd better buy him after all my trouble."

"Just ride him," Longarm said, "and we've got a deal."

About ten minutes later when Moses was saddled and bridled Diamondback mounted the mule and rode him around and around in a corral. He whipped the mule several times for no good reason other than to display his own meanness. "See," Diamondback crowed, "I told you he was a good animal. Even a damned kid could ride this mule. You seen enough?"

"I believe that I have," Longarm answered, watching Gassy out of the corner of his eye.

Diamondback dismounted then removed his hat and used it to and slap Moses hard across the face. The mule jerked back and began to bray and try to pull free. Diamondback got mad and started to jerk and kick the mule in the ribs. That's when Gassy raised the Winchester and took aim.

"Stop it!" Longarm said, knowing he had to do something or Gassy was going to shoot Diamondback dead. "That mule doesn't deserve such bad treatment. What the hell is the matter with you anyway?"

In reply, Diamondback tried to strike Moses again, but the mule broke free and started running around and around in the small corral with Diamondback hot on his heels screaming, waving his hat and cussing.

Longarm gave the man a minute. Diamondback was too drunk and slow to catch the mule and wasn't capable of doing the animal any more harm. Then suddenly, the mule stopped and charged Diamondback with his ears laid back flat on his head.

Diamondback saw his mistake too late. He clawed for his six-gun as he tried to reach the fence, but Gassy's mule caught and bit him in the back of the neck. Diamondback screamed and dove through the rails, probably saving his life. When he got clear of the corral, the man was in such a fit of pain and rage that he drew his gun and started to shoot Moses.

"No!" Longarm shouted, reaching for his own gun as Diamondback's first bullet went wide of its mark and the mule took off running.

Gassy fired just an instant later and his aim was true. Longarm saw Diamondback's mouth fly open as he struck the fence. Gassy shot him a second time in the back and the thief toppled headfirst through the railing to hang there with his legs on one side of the pole corral and his head and arms on the other side.

"Dammit, Gassy, you killed him," Longarm swore.

"Yep."

Gassy went up to Diamondback and grabbed the man's boots. He farted, then pulled Diamondback out from between the rails and spit a stream of tobacco juice in the dead man's face. "This son of a bitch shot me and then was going to shoot Moses! He deserved what he got."

"I can't argue with that," Longarm said, catching a glimpse out of the corner of his eye of a man running hard toward them.

Longarm swung around to see Diamondback's partner coming with a gun in each of his fists. Longarm raised his own gun as the man opened fire, screaming in rage.

A bullet splintered a wooden rail beside Longarm. Longarm took an instant to steady his aim and then he shot the charging man through the heart. He didn't have to waste a second bullet. The partner was dead on his feet. His arms and legs seemed to spin out of control and he crashed to the earth twitching and kicking.

"Well, Gassy, damned if we didn't kill them both."

"Good riddance!" Gassy swore, leaning against the railing and holding his side.

"How bad are you hit this time?" Longarm asked the older man as he retrieved his Winchester from the old man.

"Not bad, Marshal. Not so bad that I won't live to spit on both of their graves!"

Longarm didn't doubt that for a moment. He examined Gassy's new bullet wound and pronounced that Gassy would go on living and that the wound was hardly more than a scratch.

"Hey!" Potter shouted, coming up to them with a shotgun and staring at the two bodies. "What the hell is going on here?"

"These men robbed the old-timer, stealing everything he owned, including that mule," Longarm said. "We just sort of delivered justice."

"Says who?" Potter demanded.

Longarm knew that he had been boxed into a corner and there was no choice now except to reveal that he was a federal marshal. "Says me. I'm United States Deputy Marshal Custis Long."

Potter lowered the shotgun and stared at the badge. His eyes kept shifting back and forth between the two dead men and Longarm's shiny federal badge. Finally, he blurted, "And the government made you ride a *mule* into Canyon City?"

"It's a long story," Longarm replied. "But the short of it is that these two men robbed, almost killed Gassy and then stole his mule and left him for dead. Whatever gear they left here belongs to Gassy."

Potter's eyes shuttered and you could almost see him calculating if he could gain some financial benefit from the dead men. "They left a pack saddle and some things in my keeping and I could put them toward the board of that mule."

"Give whatever they left here to Gassy."

Potter threw up his hands in protest, "But, Marshal Long, they owe me a full day's board on that mule."

Not wanting to get into an argument over money, Longarm paid the board bill out of his own pocket and said to Gassy, "Let's get that fresh bullet crease cleaned up. Afterward, you can come back and collect Moses and your things."

But that didn't satisfy Gassy. "Not before I get back all my money and weapons."

Longarm didn't even have a chance to argue the point because Gassy fell upon the two dead men like a vulture on carrion. He emptied their pockets of a lot of cash, especially from the smaller man who had just

85

done so well at cards. He also took their gunbelts, knives and pocket watches.

"Marshal, did they steal *all* that from that old man?" Potter asked with obvious skepticism.

"I expect that they did," Longarm lied. "They took everything Gassy owned. Did they have horses?"

"Nope," Potter said, watching as Gassy counted his newfound cash. "That pair just walked into my stables leading the mule."

"Well," Longarm said, as Gassy finishing picking the bodies clean of anything they had of value including a couple of gold rings, "then I guess the debt has been settled fair and square."

Gassy was grinning broadly as he asked, "Potter, you got a couple of gunnysacks that I can put my stuff in to carry?"

"Sure. But they'll cost you ten cents each."

Gassy laughed and gave Potter fifty cents. "And I'll be takin' my mule from you now and goin' prospectin'."

"What about those bodies?" Potter cried. "They gotta be boxed and buried."

Longarm was tired of spending his money and now that Gassy had made a killing in more ways than one, he said to the old man, "You pay for their burial."

"When hell freezes over I will!"

Longarm reached out and placed a firm hand on Gassy's shoulder. "It'll cost you the value of one of those pistols you just picked off Diamondback. Now you'll do it or you and me are going to cross horns and you don't want that to happen. Do you?"

Gassy looked up at Longarm and slowly shook his head. "What are you going to do with that big black mule of yours?"

"I don't know."

"I'll buy him from you now that I have plenty of money."

"Fifty dollars and Ugly is yours."

"Thirty."

"Forty dollars," Longarm bargained, "and you've stole yourself one hell of a fine mule."

Gassy glanced over to the corral where Ugly stood watching them. The old man's eyes sort of went soft with admiration and he gladly paid Longarm the forty dollars.

"And the funeral costs," Longarm reminded Gassy.

"Aw, all right. But they're going to be planted six feet under in cheap pine boxes without any words from the Bible. And when it's done, I'll piss on both of their graves!"

"You do that," Longarm said. He turned to Potter. "And now there is you."

Potter recoiled with genuine fear. "What about me, Marshal? I didn't do anything wrong."

"Not so far you haven't. But if you let anyone in this town know that I'm a lawman I'll come back here and shoot you in the head."

"What kind of a lawman are you?" Potter cried in horror.

"One that says what he means and means what he says," Longarm replied, his eyes tightening at the corners. "So do you completely understand me?"

"Yes."

"Good," Longarm said. "Because you and Gassy are the only ones in this whole town that know I'm a lawman. And it better stay that way."

His warning was not only for Potter, but for Gassy as well.

But the old man wasn't listening. He was already hurrying off to comfort his fine pair of mules.

Longarm turned on his heel and headed back into town satisfied that justice had been swift and more than just.

Chapter 11

Even in a town as wild and lawless as Canyon City the word spread rapidly about the tall stranger who had gunned down Diamondback and another fella over the disputed ownership of an ugly mule. The few people with idle time on their hands went to see the bodies and several of them even hiked up to the cemetery hoping that they could learn more details about the shootings and the tall man with the gun on his left hip turned butt forward.

Unlike Gassy, who held forth and enjoyed his notoriety in the saloons for the next few days after the quick but much talked about burial of Diamondback and his sidekick, Longarm wasn't happy about becoming an instant celebrity. So he decided that the best thing he could do was to buy a real horse and ride on down to the San Carlos Indian Reservation. He would follow Canyon Creek and therefore have a firsthand look at the prospecting activity and what was going on among the angry Apache.

"Marshal, maybe you'd like me to go with you," Gassy said the last evening that Longarm was staying in Canyon City. "After all, we make a pretty deadly team."

"I'm not looking to kill anyone down there," Longarm told the old prospector. "And besides, we both know that the Apache love to eat *mule* meat."

"Yeah," Gassy said with a nervous gulp. "You're right. I just couldn't take the chance that they might want to shoot and eat Moses or Ugly."

"What you need to do," Longarm said, "is what you came to do and that is to prospect."

"Well," Gassy said, cutting a quiet one that he hoped would sort of float past Longarm undetected, "I been askin' around, but all the good claims are taken clear down to the reservation. From what I hear there are twenty or thirty prospectors working at the north end of the reservation and doin' pretty good. But I figured . . . what with you being sympathetic to the Apache and a lawman besides . . . that you wouldn't like it much if I started to prospecting on Indian lands."

"You've got that much right. And, when I see those prospectors, I'll tell them to get off the reservation. That's just the kind of thing that is going to cause big trouble."

Longarm and Gassy were standing in the shadows just outside of the saloon when a woman appeared from between the buildings. She was tall, dressed in a dark dress with a long scarf tied tight under her chin. "Mister," she said, to Longarm, "I need to speak to you alone."

The light was poor, but even so Longarm could see that the woman was most likely either a Mexican or a half-breed and really quite beautiful with high cheekbones, raven-black hair and a fine figure. She was somewhat mysterious and his interest was piqued even though his first impression was that she was a prostitute hoping to take his money.

"Miss," he said, "although you are quite beautiful, I'm not interested in what you have to sell tonight. Sorry."

"You are too quick to judge because I'm not selling anything," she said, her voice leaving no doubt that she was offended by Longarm's snap judgment. "I think that you are a man who badly needs some advice. I came to give it to you free."

Gassy scrubbed the gray stubble on his chin and studied the woman for a minute before he said, "Lady, I've got five dollars and you can come out into the wood with me and give me all the advice you want."

Her eyes flashed. "Go away, you stupid, smelly old man!"

Gassy blinked and Longarm had to suppress a smile. "Gassy," he said, "I think this lady wants you to go away. I'll be leaving town early tomorrow. But I'll most likely return to Canyon City in a few days. Just take care of yourself and those mules."

"I'll do 'er," Gassy said, cutting a vicious fart to show that his feelings were injured and to get even with the tall, dark woman.

"Let's move off a bit to clear the air," Longarm said, walking a dozen feet before he stopped to wait.

"Why do you keep that man's company when he smells worse than any skunk?" she asked, wrinkling her nose in displeasure.

"It's complicated," Longarm said. "What did you mean about giving me some advice?"

"They know who you are."

"What are you talking about?"

"The people who own this town and run things know that you are a federal marshal and that you have come to settle the trouble between my people and these whites." The woman looked directly into Longarm's eyes. "I thought you should know that they want to kill you."

"Who are these people?" Longarm asked. "Give me their names."

"I cannot."

Longarm could tell by the way she answered that she was not going to change her mind. "Who are *you*?"

"I am not important."

"But you're not a white woman."

"I am Apache and some Mexican. Mostly Apache."

"And what do you do here in Canyon City?"

"You ask too many questions," she told him bluntly.

"Can I at least ask you your name?"

"Donita." She hesitated, looked around to make sure that no one was watching or listening. "Senorita Donita Ramirez."

"Well, senorita, I'm leaving tomorrow morning for the reservation."

"Perhaps you will not."

Longarm frowned. "What is that supposed to mean?"

Donita was slow to answer and she was growing increasingly nervous. "Maybe I made a mistake by talking to you. If I were seen here with you then . . . I had better go right now."

"Wait!" Longarm grabbed her arm which was surprisingly muscular. Donita looked down at his hand and the meaning was clear. *Let go of me.*

He released the mysterious woman. "I have to know if someone wants me dead tonight."

"Yes."

"Do you know if they intend to come to my hotel room or . . ."

Donita shook her head. "I do not know when they will come. Only that your life is in great danger and you must be very careful. You should leave this town while you still can."

Longarm sensed that he was probably not going to learn much more so he said, "I thank you for your warning, Miss Ramirez. Will I ever have the good fortune to see you again?"

"I do not think so."

"Is there someone at the San Carlos Reservation that can help me find the truth? Who will help me and that I can trust?"

Donita nodded. "My father. Mankiller. You can trust him. Tell him that I am still well and will try to come soon."

Longarm didn't understand. "What do you mean? If you want to leave this town then come with me tomorrow. I will protect you from whatever you are afraid of."

She studied his face for a moment, then shook her head. "You have no idea what you are saying."

"I am saying you can come with me in the morning . . . if that is what you want to do."

Her dark eyes clouded with sadness. "More than anything. But . . . but I cannot."

Longarm wanted to ask her why not, but Donita

turned and hurried off into the darkness. He stood there for several moments wondering who she was and what was the meaning of her warning. Longarm found it very disturbing that Donita Ramirez knew that he was a federal marshal. If she knew, then that meant either Potter or Gassy had betrayed his trust. If Longarm were to bet on it, he would bet that Potter had been the one who had given away his identity as a federal marshal. He'd been angry about not getting to keep and then sell the belongings of Diamondback and his friend. And to break Longarm's trust might well be the way he had sought his small revenge.

Longarm went back to his hotel room and paced the small floor for several moments before making a decision. He would heed Donita's warning and leave right now for the San Carlos Reservation. He had already bought a horse and saddle and told Potter that he would be departing early in the morning.

Instead, he would show up at Potter's Stable, saddle his new mount and be long gone before anyone who meant to kill him even had a chance to act.

His decision made, Longarm packed his few belongings, checked his gun and rifle, then left the hotel walking quickly to the stables.

"Potter!" he called into the darkness.

Longarm had to call out the man's name several times before Potter emerged from a little shack behind his barn. He was dressed in a rumpled nightshirt. In the lamplight that seeped out through the doorway behind him, Longarm saw a very fat and naked woman clutching a half empty bottle of whiskey.

"What do you want at this hour?" Potter demanded.

"I'm leaving *now*," Longarm told the liveryman. "Hurry up and get dressed. Unlock the room where my saddle is hanging so that I can saddle and bridle my horse."

"It's late. Come back tomorrow morning!" Potter protested. "I . . . I got a friend with me and . . ."

"Yeah," Longarm said, "I can see your friend and I can see that she is the kind that will wait. So get dressed and stop arguing with me."

"Tell you what," Potter said, glancing back over his shoulder at the cow standing in his doorway, "I'll unlock the saddle room and you get your own horse saddled. Then you ride out of here and you don't come back. How does that sound?"

Longarm wanted to reach out and grab Potter by the throat. Instead, he said, "Fine. Give me the key and get back to your whore."

"Who's callin' me a whore?" the woman cried, having overheard Longarm. "You got no right to call me anything, you cold-blooded killer! What kind of a gawdamn lawman do you think you are?"

The last thing that Longarm wanted was to get in a shouting match with a drunken prostitute so that half the town could hear them fighting. So he grabbed Potter, spun him completely around and shoved him at the shack with such force that the man staggered and almost pitched headfirst into the yard.

Longarm was furious. Even the whore knew he was a federal marshal and there was little doubt that Potter was the one with the big mouth. "Hurry up with the key and tell that . . . that woman friend of yours to get back inside and shut the door!"

The woman heard this order and started swearing, but Potter had been given enough of a scare to run up to her and push her inside. Minutes later, the stable-man came out to Longarm with a lantern and a key. "Don't start no fire. There's a lot of straw and hay in my barn so be damned careful."

Longarm took the lantern and key without replying. He could hear Potter and the woman loudly arguing inside the shack a moment before its door slammed shut for the second time.

Longarm didn't like or trust Potter, but if the stable-man was working as an informant for an enemy, then the man wouldn't have time to give away the fact that Longarm was on his way out of town in the dead of the night.

Longarm grabbed the best saddle in the saddle room and also the best blanket and bridle. He wasn't sure if they were the ones that he had bought, but he didn't really care. Potter had set someone on him. Someone powerful and determined that no federal in-terference should be meddling in the business of Canyon City.

"If they come onto the reservation after me I will be looking over my back trail and I'll kill them," Lon-garm vowed as he quickly saddled the tall roan geld-ing he had bought only a day earlier. "And I'll find out why Miss Ramirez can't come home to her people. To her father, Mankiller."

The roan seemed awfully narrow after Longarm had become accustomed to his powerful Missouri mule. Longarm almost wished he still had Ugly, but the animal was in good hands now and what was needed was some speed to get out of Canyon City be-fore anyone was the wiser.

The roan was fast and as Longarm galloped out of town he heard a coyote howl in the night. Maybe it was a good sign, but maybe it was a bad omen. One way or the other he was about to find out.

Chapter 12

Longarm followed Canyon Creek until the going became so treacherous that he stopped for the night and slept until daybreak hidden deep in the pines. With the first light of dawn he awoke and continued following the creek seeing clusters of prospectors working in the cold, swift currents. Sometimes they looked up at him and waved in a half-hearted greeting, but most of the time they showed a distinct measure of unfriendliness. Several of them hurried over to their rifles and their message to stay away from the claims that they were working could not have been clearer.

That afternoon Longarm came upon an excited young man who was leading a burro back towards Canyon City as fast as it would run. His face was flushed with exertion and he looked pale and shaken.

"What's the hurry?" Longarm asked from the top of his roan.

"The Apache attacked a camp about five miles downstream. Murdered at least five prospectors. Scalped 'em and shot their animals, then stole everything they owned."

Longarm swore under his breath realizing that he

might be too little too late to stop another Indian war. The killing had already begun and it was doubtful that anything he could do would stop a war. "Were you with the five when they were attacked?"

"If I had been I sure as hell wouldn't be talking to you right now," the young prospector shouted.

"Take it easy," Longarm said, deciding that the prospector was very near to going crazy with fear. "And you'd better slow down or you'll kill that burro."

"Better him than me."

Longarm dismounted wishing he had some whiskey to give the terrified man. "Tell me exactly what happened."

"I was working downstream about a mile and my camp was hidden in some rocks."

"So you were alone?"

"Yes! The Apache must have ridden right past me last night and struck the next camp at daybreak."

"Did you hear gunshots?"

"Of course I did!"

"And I assume you stayed hidden until the fighting was over."

His face flushed with anger. "Mister, if you're suggesting that I should have gone to help those five you're out of your damned mind. I could hear them screaming and it curdled my blood. There was nothing I could have done to save those five prospectors!"

"Did you hear the Indians screaming?"

"No, but hearing those men being murdered was bad enough."

"I know that," Longarm said calmly. "And you did the right thing to stay hidden until the danger past. There was no sense in throwing your life away in a lost cause."

100

The young man vigorously nodded in agreement. "That's the way I saw it. I'm lucky to be alive and you'd better turn that horse around and head on back to Canyon City with me. Those Apache could be putting us in their rifle sights at this very moment."

As if to emphasize his point the young man shaded his eyes with the flat of his hand and gazed anxiously back downstream. He was sweating profusely even though it was cool. "They're probably up in the rocks hiding someplace. It ain't healthy to work the stream down this far south."

"Were you panning gold on their reservation?" Longarm asked, trying to make the question seem unimportant.

"Hell if I know. Who cares, anyway?"

"The San Carlos Apache obviously do."

"Mister, there ain't no sign or nothin' tellin' a man where the reservation line is drawn. But I was probably working the stream at the top of the reservation. I don't know. It doesn't *matter*. The only thing I want to do is get back to Canyon City and warn the people there that the Indians are on the warpath. They might even be coming to hit the town and kill everyone."

"I doubt that," Longarm said. "Did you actually see the attack on the five prospectors?"

"Hell, no! I saw the bodies a couple of hours after it was finished and that was enough." He passed his hands over his eyes and his body was shaking with fear and from the horror of what he had been forced to witness. "I won't ever forget the sight of those men. The Apache left them . . ."

The young man couldn't finish. He retched and retched, but there was nothing in his stomach and all he had was the dry heaves.

Longarm would have liked to have asked the young man more questions about the attack, but it was clear that he was so upset and scared that he wouldn't have given the time or been of much use.

The prospector grabbed the lead rope to his burro and jerked it hard in the direction of Canyon City. "You'd better come with me, mister! You'd better turn that roan around and hightail it with me for Canyon City. Our odds are better if we're together than separated."

"I'm going on down to take a look at the bodies," Longarm said, reining his gelding around and continuing downstream.

"Mister, you're crazy! I'm telling you that death is waiting down there. Don't make yourself number six!"

"I'll sure try not to," Longarm shouted back up the canyon as he continued on downstream.

It was almost sunset when he came upon the five dead prospectors and had to scare away the swarming turkey vultures. Longarm tied his roan in the pines. He took his rifle and crept up to the edge of the prospector camp and studied the bloody carnage with the big birds circling low overhead or sitting in distant trees eagerly waiting a return to their feasting.

The five miners had definitely been caught by surprise early in the morning because three of them were still dressed in their woolen long johns and barefooted. The other pair was sprawled off a ways and it seemed clear that they had been gathering wood for a fire probably to heat coffee and some breakfast.

All of the bodies had been scalped and mutilated. They were covered with dried blood and a black cloud of blowflies swarmed over each of them. The stench of death was already sickening.

Longarm noted two things of special interest. The most obvious being the iron-shod tracks of horses that had trampled the campground. Indians didn't make a habit of having shoes on their ponies. White men always shod their horses. That told Longarm one of two things. Either the five prospectors owned shod horses that had stampeded through the camp during the fight . . . or the attackers were not Indians, but rather whites posing as murdering, scalping San Carlos Apache.

After about a half hour of studying every detail of the death camp from a distance of about fifty feet Longarm crept in for a close-up view. He knew that he had to hurry because the sun was just gilding the edges of the canyon and the shadows were growing darker.

The first dead prospector he came upon was dressed in tattered long johns. He was tall and thin with a full beard and his eyes were staring up at the darkening sky. Longarm knelt beside the corpse and inspected the body carefully. This one had been shot at least four times before he'd been scalped and mutilated.

Longarm moved on to do a quick study of the other bodies. The scalping of all five men was not only barbaric, but extremely crude work. So crude that it almost led Longarm to think that these men had been scalped either by a very dull knife or perhaps even the blade of a tool such as a shovel.

Longarm inspected what remained in the camp's tent. The pots and pans were still present, none taken. Weapons were missing as was cash. But the prospector's boots were all to be found and so were their belts and knives.

Reservation Indians would have taken such useful items as boots, belts and knives, he mused.

Longarm had been so focused on his inspection that he hadn't even heard or noticed another small group of turkey vultures squabbling about two hundred yards away. Longarm hurried over to scare the carrion birds off and that is when he saw several bloody scalps wedged in between the rocks. The scalps had been thrown away and the large scavengers had obviously been struggling in vain to reach them.

"Apache didn't do this," Longarm concluded as night fell. "Apache would have done a far better job scalping and they'd have kept the scalps as trophies. And they'd have collected some of the best pots and pans as well as the boots. This was carried out by murdering whites."

Longarm buried the bloody scalps with rocks so that the vultures wouldn't ever be able to reach them. "This all adds up to white men murdering these five and then trying to make it look like the work of reservation Indians."

Longarm went back to the camp where there was no shortage of worn picks and shovels. He would have preferred to have loaded the bodies on horses and taken them back to Canyon City where he would have proven to an audience of townsfolk that these men had not been murdered by Apache. But he had no horses to transport the stiff and already decaying corpses, so the only thing to do was to bury them as fast as possible.

Longarm chose as their cemetery a little grassy place not more than fifty feet from the stream. If this stream flooded in the spring then the corpses might rise in the tide and that would be pretty gruesome. But everywhere else he looked to dig he found the ground flinty and hard with rock. Longarm hated pick and shovel work and he gave himself a break by the choosing soft, rock-free ground under the grass.

He set to work and dug all five of the graves in less than two hours using only the starlight. Then he dragged the bodies over to the graves, rolled them into their resting places and covered them each with at least three feet of damp dirt. As a final touch and salve to his conscience, he covered the five graves with a layer of large river rocks hoping that this would keep bears and other animals from digging up and devouring the bodies.

It was after midnight when he finished the hard, distasteful work and he fell exhausted on his blankets back in the trees. The stars overhead twinkled brightly and he heard an owl hooting somewhere in the dark forest.

What was he to do tomorrow? He could press on to the San Carlos Reservation headquarters and tell the people in charge there about this deadly deception . . . or he could turn his horse around and go back to Canyon City and try to defuse what would surely be panic and misguided revenge.

Longarm wasn't sure which course he should take. Both seemed very urgent and important. He decided that he would get some sleep and when rested make the decision tomorrow morning.

Either option seemed about as prudent and safe as jumping off a tall cliff.

Chapter 13

Longarm had only to ride a mile south of town before he saw where the whites were working furiously in an effort to divert Canyon Creek away from the reservation. In a few more miles and after riding onto the reservation he began to see brush houses scattered here and there as the steep canyons surrounding the creek fell away and the valley widened.

A little deeper onto the reservation he began to notice small Apache farms and ranches. If the Apache saw Longarm, they did not feel threatened by one white horseman and did not come to investigate.

In time, the little game trail that he'd been following for miles along Canyon Creek became a wagon track and then a well-traveled dirt road. Longarm followed it until he saw distant buildings and an American flag flying from a tall, white flagpole.

This, he knew, would be the reservation headquarters and the place where he would find white officials in charge. He had forgotten to ask his boss in Denver who the officials were and if anything was known about their background, efficiency or integrity, but

Longarm figured he'd find the answers to those questions soon enough.

When he rode into the military-like compound a half dozen tough-looking Apache came out to block his path.

"I'm a United States marshal," he said, having no idea if they would understand him or not. To make sure that they did understand, Longarm showed them his badge. One of the Apache, a short man with a barrel chest, spoke to the others and they motioned that he was to dismount.

"Follow me," the leader said.

"What about my horses and gear?"

"Apache not steal from white lawman."

"You wouldn't happen to be Mankiller, would you?"

The Apache's eyes shadowed and then he raised his hand to point to a brush remuda under which sat several old Apache. "Mankiller."

"I have a message to deliver to him."

But the Apache waved this request off and made it clear that Longarm was to follow him into the reservation headquarters.

The headquarters were by far the most impressive structure that Longarm had yet seen on the San Carlos Indian Reservation. It was large and built of heavy logs. It had a long, wide porch where there must have been a dozen handmade chairs. Longarm could well imagine that the chairs were for the white officials, their wives and friends.

Before he entered the headquarters building Longarm turned a complete circle as he studied every detail about the reservation headquarters. There were at least ten outbuildings including several barns and corrals.

This place had been an early military post. Even as he was studying the compound several soldiers came out of a barracks and stood gazing in his direction.

As Longarm stepped up on the porch a slovenly sergeant with unshined boots, a three-day growth of beard and his tunic hanging out of his pants stepped into his path.

"Who are you and what do you want?" the sergeant demanded.

"I'm a United States marshal sent here from Denver to investigate the troubles you're having over the water flowing down Canyon Creek."

"We don't need any help from outsiders."

"That isn't for you to decide, Sergeant."

The soldier obviously didn't appreciate that remark, but Longarm didn't care. He pulled out his badge for the second time that day.

The sergeant stared at it and frowned. "What the hell is this about?"

"That's none of your business. Now take me to see the man in charge of this reservation."

From somewhere within the dim interior of the headquarters, a voice barked, "Who the hell is it, Sergeant?"

"Wait here a minute."

Longarm leaned against a porch post and waited almost five minutes before the sergeant reappeared and motioned him inside. "Captain Norman has consented to see you now."

He'd damn well better consent to see me, Longarm thought.

He was ushered into the captain's spacious and well-appointed office. The furniture was heavy and probably made by skilled Apache craftsmen. The walls were decorated with Apache weapons and mounted heads of deer, elk and even a mountain lion. But it was Norman himself that commanded the most attention. He was a tall, silver-haired man with a long, slanted jaw and a hooked nose. His hair was cropped very short and his eyes were a strange blue-green color not unlike the turquoise stones that the Navajo and Zuni Indians favored for their jewelry.

"You've come a long way, Marshal. Why don't you sit down and take a load off your feet."

"Thank you," Longarm said.

"Sergeant, pour us two glasses of my best whiskey."

Longarm nodded his head in appreciation and not a word was spoken until their crystal glasses were filled. Then Norman raised his glass in a toast and said, "To better times, Marshal."

"To better times."

The whiskey was as good as Longarm had ever been able to find in all of Denver and his throat was dry from the dust and long journey down from Canyon City.

"Excellent whiskey," he told Norman as he drained his glass.

Norman drained his as well and then ordered the sergeant to refill their glasses one more time. That done, the captain said, "I assume you are here because of the friction that has sprung up between my Apache and the people of Canyon Creek."

"*Your* Apache?"

From the suddenly changed expression on his face Longarm could see that Captain Norman wasn't a man who liked or was even accustomed to having his words dissected. "Marshal, what I said was simply a figure of speech and nothing more. Now state your business."

Longarm told the captain about how word of the conflict over water had gone all the way to Washington D.C. and then boomeranged back to Denver. He ended by saying, "The Indian wars are over, Captain Norman. The Apache were the last holdouts and the toughest to fight. There isn't anyone that wants to see a conflict between the Apache and the whites replayed. This country has enough troubles just rebuilding the South and taking care of its citizens."

"I couldn't agree more," Norman said. "And so far we've been able to keep a lid on things here at the San Carlos. I am completely confident that this water disagreement is something that will all blow over in the very near future. I think that Washington and your superiors in Denver have badly overreacted and you must tell them so at once. Trust me; I have everything under control at this end."

Longarm had a strong urge to grab and shake this complacent fool. "So you're saying that no blood has been shed between the San Carlos Apache and the whites?"

"That's *exactly* what I'm saying." Norman leaned back in his office chair and lit a cigar. "Of course I realize that there is a *potential* for trouble. There is always that when you are dealing with savages. However, we treat them well here and I have explained to their leaders that the people of Canyon City do have a prior right to Canyon Creek."

"Meaning you believe that it was diverted to this reservation illegally?"

"Of course it was." Norman blew a cloud of cigar

smoke into the air and smiled condescendingly. "You're an outsider so I understand the ignorance of that question."

Longarm felt an anger building deep inside. "Captain, I'm curious to know how long this reservation has existed."

Norman's patronizing smile evaporated. "What has that got to do with our discussion?"

"I'm not an attorney of law," Longarm answered, "but I think that if the river was diverted naturally and before the reservation was established, then the new river course onto the reservation is the one that would be found legal . . . not some prior watercourse changed long ago by nature."

Captain Norman steepled his fingers. "You are not a lawyer, correct?"

"I just said that."

"Then any supposition on your part is worthless, Marshal. And furthermore, that kind of talk has the potential of inflaming the situation, not healing it."

"I rode onto this reservation this morning and saw many small Apache ranches and farms."

"The farms are total failures," Norman snapped. "The Apache do not have the stomach for plowing and harvesting. I will admit that they are passable livestock managers and seem to be doing especially well with horses, sheep and goats."

"The farms I saw had corn and cotton growing and they must need the water from Canyon Creek or their fields will dry up."

"Let them! As I've already pointed out, Apaches are not nor will they ever be crop farmers."

"And what about the hay fields that they need to keep their animals alive through the winter? Captain,

112

this is high, rugged country. You must get a considerable amount of snow at this elevation, so I'm sure they do need to raise their own hay and store it for winter."

Norman jumped to his feet and stabbed his cigar at Longarm. "You, sir, are nothing but a marshal. You're not an agriculturalist. Not a lawyer and certainly not an expert on the Apache."

"Nor are you," Longarm said flatly.

"How dare you!"

Longarm could see that this meeting was about to come to an end and he was angry. "I dare plenty. And I'll tell you something else, Captain. While you sit here in this office thinking that no blood has been shed between the whites and *your Apache* I stand to correct you on that misconception. Because just last night five white men were murdered and scalped on this reservation!"

Norman fell back in his chair, eyes widening. He whispered, "Nonsense."

"I can take you to the death camp where they were attacked and murdered. Why don't you have the sergeant saddle you up a horse and come with me for a ride? Or are you the kind of lazy armchair overseer that I take you for?"

Norman glared at Longarm. If looks could kill, Longarm knew he would be dead. And it took a minute or two for Norman to regain enough composure to finally stammer, "By God I will come and see this camp where you claim my Apache slaughtered five whites! Sergeant!"

The sergeant stuck his head in the door so fast that Longarm knew the man had been hanging just outside the door listening to every word spoken. "Yes, sir, Captain?"

"Sergeant, saddle my horse and your own as well. We will be going for a ride."

"How far, sir?"

Longarm had the answer. "Not far. Maybe fifteen miles. We can be there and back before sundown."

The sergeant looked to his captain and then said, "We might need to take some of our scouts. I could order a few Apache as well as soldiers to ride with us."

"Sergeant," the captain said, "that is an excellent idea. Any objections, Marshal?"

"Not a one."

"Then you'll have to excuse me while I make my preparations."

"Sure," Longarm said. "Mind if I go over to your mess hall and get something to eat?"

"Help yourself."

"I will," Longarm said, angry and offended by the thoughtlessness of this man. Captain Norman, it seemed clear, was an officious fool. A man who thought that he was in charge when he really didn't have a clue as to the trouble that was about to turn this country into a bloodbath.

Chapter 14

Mankiller was the leader of the Apache scouts and Longarm judged the warrior to be in his mid-fifties. He was short and stocky like most Apache and wore a shirt without sleeves. Mankiller's arms were ropy with muscle and heavily scarred while his legs were thick, but seemed too short for his powerful body.

"I pass on greetings from your daughter, Senorita Ramirez," Longarm whispered when they stopped to rest their horses.

Mankiller didn't even acknowledge the message, much less ask about his daughter. Longarm, however, was not surprised by this because Apache were known for their stoic expressions. "She is well."

Mankiller's eyes met his for only the briefest of moments and then the Apache leader went to care for his horse.

"You're wastin' your time trying to strike up a conversation with old Mankiller or any of his friends," the sergeant said as he joined Longarm. "They speak pidgin English, but they don't let on that they do."

Longarm looked up at the sky and saw dark clouds on the horizon. "Maybe it'll storm this evening," he said.

"Yeah, it does that a lot this time of year," the sergeant replied.

They mounted up and continued on toward the death camp. Up ahead, Longarm could see vultures circling and so he knew that was where the slaughter had taken place.

"Sergeant," Captain Norman said, "tell the men to keep a sharp eye out for renegade Apache snipers."

"Yes, sir!"

When they reached the death camp, Longarm dismounted and showed the soldiers what he had found and where he had buried the five bodies. "If you doubt that they were killed," he said, "you could have your men dig up the graves."

"I'll take your word for it," Captain Norman said.

"Their scalps were tossed over in those rocks," Longarm said. "And from the looks of 'em, I'm pretty sure that they weren't the work of Indians."

"Are you an expert on the fine art of scalping?" Norman asked.

"No," Longarm replied. "But before your men wipe out these tracks, look at them closely. You'll see that these horses were shod. Everything here points to white men ambushing and killing white men, but trying to make it look like the work of Indians."

Captain Norman didn't say anything. He had dismounted and handed his reins to a private; he was now stalking around the scene of the slaughter, head down and brow furrowed with concentration.

Finally, the captain said, "I'm not sure that I agree

with you, Marshal Long. Many Apache ride shod horses."

"Is that a fact?"

Norman nodded vigorously. "It certainly is. For example, my scout's horses are *all* shod."

Longarm wasn't convinced. "That's because they're riding army horses. And what about the poor job of scalping?"

"The killers were obviously in a big hurry." Captain Norman called, "Mankiller?"

The Apache leader rode his pony over to join them. "What do the signs tell you happened here?"

Mankiller slid off his pony and said, "White people kill white men then ride up that canyon to leave reservation."

"Ha!" Captain Norman laughed as he turned to Longarm. "I really didn't expect an Apache to say another Apache did this killing."

Norman shaded his eyes and studied the canyon. "Tell me, Mankiller, do you think that these whites are still in that canyon?"

Mankiller shrugged to indicate that he did not know. Longarm thought it interesting that he also did not volunteer to ride up the canyon to find out.

"Captain, maybe we should dig up those bodies and take them into town for a proper burial," the sergeant suggested.

The captain considered this for a moment and then said, "Yes. That would be the proper thing to do."

Longarm objected. "Why? All you'll accomplish is to stir up the people of Canyon City. Bringing those bodies into town will cause a panic or a backlash that will start a war."

"The victims deserve a Christian burial," the captain insisted. "But that is not to say that we don't appreciate you taking care of them by digging each a shallow grave. Sergeant?"

"Yes, sir?"

"Have the men dig up the bodies, wrap them in blankets or canvas and then lash them onto the backs of their horses. We'll deliver them to Canyon City and stay there overnight. We'll come back to the reservation headquarters tomorrow."

The sergeant nodded and set about to carry out these orders.

Longarm was angry with the captain and stepped into the man's path. "And have you given any thought to the safety of your scouts?"

"What do you mean?"

"If they ride into Canyon City in the wake of these killings, I think that their lives might be in grave danger, Captain."

"Mankiller and the others can take care of themselves."

"Maybe so in the rough country. But when you bring in those dead men there will be a lot of anger and it could be turned on your own scouts. I don't think having them in Canyon City is a good idea at all."

Captain Norman's lips tightened at the corners. "Marshal Long, what you think or do not think is of no importance. Now that you've done your job and I've thanked you for both burying the five men and for reporting their deaths to me at headquarters, your usefulness is over. I suggest that when we get back to town that you make arrangements to return to Denver."

Longarm could not believe what he was hearing. "Captain, just as you don't put any weight to my thoughts and opinions, so I do not care to hear your suggestions. I've been sent here on official business and I assure you that I will not leave until this dispute and trouble is over."

"Very well," Norman said in a dismissive tone, "but, if you cause me trouble or complicate matters, then I will make sure you are arrested and deported. Is that clear?"

Longarm dipped his chin and remounted his horse. He would ride back to Canyon City and start asking questions. He'd find everything he could about Captain Norman and about his role in this matter. One thing for sure, Norman was a fool and Longarm had the feeling he might also be corrupt.

He just wished that Mankiller trusted and would confide in him so that he could get a better handle on Captain Norman.

When Longarm galloped into Canyon City he immediately went looking for the mayor of the town, a man named Merle Watson. He found Watson shooting pool in a tent along with a barber and the town's undertaker.

"Mayor," Longarm said, coming right up to the man, "my name is Custis Long and I'm a deputy United States marshal sent here from Denver to try and work things out peacefully between your town and the San Carlos Apache."

Merle Watson was a fat man with mutton-chop whiskers and a flowery silk vest. He scowled at Longarm, blew a cloud of stinking smoke in his direction and drawled, "Ah, yes, you're the fella that gunned down Diamondback and his friend at Potter's stable a few days ago."

"I had no choice in that matter," Longarm said. "But what I want to talk to you about now is very important."

Watson raised his busy eyebrows. "And the lives of two men weren't important?"

"Look," Longarm said, "Captain Norman and his men will be riding into town within the next hour or two. And they're bringing in five scalped bodies."

Suddenly, Longarm had the rapt attention of everyone in the tent. "Did you say *scalped*?"

"I did. But I'm sure that these men were scalped by other whites. That tells me that someone stands to gain if there is open warfare between the whites and the Apache."

"Damn right someone will gain," Mayor Merle Watson snapped. "We'll kill all them murderin' Apache off and that'll be the end to this talk about giving them back their water."

"Mayor," Longarm said, watching the others bob their heads up and down in hearty agreement with the mayor's statement, "you have a responsibility to do what is fair and right. You also have a responsibility not to incite the people of Canyon City into seeking revenge against the Apache for something they did not do."

"Marshal," the barber said, pushing between them, "you seem to be on the side of the Apache. And quite frankly, that's about what we expected when we learned a marshal was being sent to Canyon City."

"I'm not on the Apache's side," Longarm argued.

"But the Indian wars are over and the government wants this dispute settled peaceably."

"Fine!" the mayor stormed. "Then tell the Apache that the damned water is gonna be ours and that's the end of the discussion."

"Mayor, if you divert that stream off their reservation, then their farms and ranches will dry up and blow away."

"Tough shit."

Longarm took a deep breath and stepped back from the men. "All right," he said, "I'm officially taking over this town."

"What!" Watson bellowed. "You can't do that!"

"Watch me," Longarm replied. "From this minute forth, I'm the one that is going to see that law and order prevails and that justice is done between this town and the San Carlos Apache."

"Mister," Watson shouted, charging forward and waving his cigar, "you are way overstepping your bounds. You have no authority. None whatsoever in Canyon City!"

"You're wrong about that," Longarm told the fat mayor and his friends. "I'm in total authority here."

"As soon as he arrives, I'll have Captain Norman and his soldiers arrest you and throw away the key."

"You'll do nothing of the kind," Longarm told the mayor. "And furthermore, if those men diverting the creek south of town aren't gone by tomorrow morning, they'll be arrested."

"And then what will you do with them?" the barber shouted. "We ain't got a jail. And those men are working under our orders."

"Your orders."

"I'm a member of the town council. So is Mr. Purvey, here. And I'll tell you something else that you don't know."

"I'm listening."

"We've had a *certified government* surveyor's report saying that the Apache redirected Canyon Creek twenty-five years ago."

"I don't believe it!" Longarm snapped.

"Doesn't matter what you believe. Only what the courts believe and we have proof."

"How much did you and your cronies pay this surveyor to lie?"

The mayor answered: "Marshal, you're way out of line. Me, George Potter and the other city council members run this town and make all the decisions. Furthermore, the only law we need down in these parts is that represented by the United States army. And I promise you that Captain Norman understands this and he will back us up to the limit. And we will be supported by the courts."

"I'd like to see that surveyor's report," Longarm said.

"Not a chance. But a judge will see it if push comes to shove. Face it, Marshal Long, we're holding all the high cards in this game and you're running a bluff."

"It's no bluff, Mayor. You've been warned," Longarm said knowing that further conversation was useless. "Tomorrow morning those men that I saw working to divert Canyon Creek had better be gone or they'll be arrested."

"You can't back up your tough talk," Watson hissed. "If Captain Norman and his men don't shoot you tomorrow morning, then one of us damn sure will!"

"A lot of fools have tried," Longarm warned as he backed out of the tent, "and a lot of fools have died."

Chapter 15

After his sharp disagreement with Mayor Watson and two other members of the city council Longarm knew that his back was up against the wall and that he would get no local support. He also knew that if he slept in Canyon City that night, he might very well be murdered or taken under military arrest by Captain Norman. Longarm couldn't be sure, but it appeared that the captain and the mayor were both sympathetic only to the greedy interests of the boomtown. Longarm also thought it very likely that Captain Norman might very well be buttering his own bread at the expense of the Apache he was charged to serve and protect. It was a sad situation not at all uncommon on the frontier.

On his way out of town to find a safe haven for the night, Longarm stopped at the local feed store and bought twenty-five pounds of oats for his roan. He had ridden the animal hard in the last few days and it looked as if that might continue.

"Hey, Custis!"

Longarm was coming out of the feed store when he saw Gassy hurrying over to talk.

"How you doin'?" Gassy asked, looking worried.

"Well," Longarm replied, "so far I've managed to antagonize both the town council and the United States army. As far as I can tell, you might be the only friend I have left in this town."

"That bad, huh?"

"You don't know the half of it," Longarm replied. "In a very short time Captain Norman from the reservation headquarters is going to be riding into this town with five dead bodies . . . all of them scalped."

"Holy hog fat!" Gassy cried. "Are the Apache on the warpath?"

"I don't think so," Longarm answered before quickly telling the old prospector about his suspicions of a setup to make it appear as if the Apache were the murderers.

"Someone in Canyon City wants a war," Longarm ended up saying. "And I'm pretty sure it's the city council."

Gassy cut a slow squeaker as he thought about this for a minute and Longarm backed up a few steps to give himself some fresh air.

Gassy said, "And you've given the town until tomorrow morning to stop trying to divert the creek away from the reservation?"

"That's right," Longarm replied.

"Well, I don't know how you're going to make that foolishness stand," Gassy said in his usual blunt manner. "This town needs that water and they won't give it up without a fight. I heard that they're only about a week away from diverting the creek so that not even a drop of water flows onto the San Carlos Reservation."

"I can't let them do that," Longarm said. "You should see those little farms and ranches on the reservation. The reservation Apache are barely making a go of it as it is now."

"I expect that's true."

"If we're ever going to expect the Indians to stay on their reservations we have to figure out a way that they can make a living instead of starving to death or depending entirely on our government's handouts."

"You ain't from Arizona so you don't understand that a lot of folks would just as soon they *all* starved. Geronimo and Cochise and their bands of renegades took a lot of white scalps not so long ago."

"I understand that, but Cochise is now dead and buried somewhere in the Dragoon Mountains," Longarm said. "And Geronimo is living on the San Carlos Reservation in peace."

"He may still be on the reservation," Gassy said, "but a lot of people think he is down in Mexico gathering men to go on the warpath again. I don't think we've seen the last of Geronimo and his warriors. Not by a damned sight we haven't."

"That could be true," Longarm conceded. "But we don't want to give Geronimo or someone like Mankiller any excuses to go on the warpath. That's why this water dispute has to be dealt with fairly."

Gassy chuckled. "Fairness ain't got nothin' to do with nothin', Marshal. You ought to know that by now."

"I do," Longarm replied. "But it's my job to try and see that some level of justice is done. And I mean to do it starting tomorrow."

"If you go down there where those men are working on Canyon Creek you'll come back in a pine box."

"Maybe," Longarm said.

"No maybe about it," Gassy insisted. "Dammit, Marshal, I sure wish you'd reconsider."

"I can't," Longarm told the old prospector. "If I back down now before the town council or Captain Norman, I'm finished here."

"So what's wrong with that? Are you gonna let pride take you to an early grave?"

Longarm patted the man on the shoulder and decided to change the subject to something more pleasant. "How are Ugly and Moses?"

"They're doin' real fine. I bought me a little freight wagon and they're makin' me a ton of money. Those two mules are as loyal to each other as brothers."

"Glad to hear it." Longarm went to his horse and tied the grain to his saddle. He had some salt bacon, beans and coffee in his pack and plenty of ammunition. "Gassy, I'm heading out of town for the night. I don't think it would be all that healthy for me to sleep in Canyon City."

"You sure got that figured right," Gassy agreed. "For what it's worth and if you're dumb enough to persist in this nonsense, I'll be down at the diversion site tomorrow morning. You saved my life and I'll back you, Marshal."

"I appreciate that," Longarm told him, "but it won't be necessary. I laid down the rules and I'll back 'em up myself."

"Well," Gassy said, looking sad, "the very least I can do then is to collect your bullet-riddled body and make sure you get a proper burial. Any next of kin that you want me to notify?"

"No," Longarm told him. "And don't look so down in the mouth. I've painted myself in worse corners and managed to survive."

"Sure," Gassy said, but he didn't sound convinced as he walked away.

That night Longarm camped about two miles west of Canyon City up in the pines where there was water and wood. He lit a small fire and cooked some bacon and warmed up his beans. He also had a bottle of one hundred proof Old Buzzard whiskey which was strong enough to dissolve boot leather. Longarm would sip sparingly of the powerful whiskey and then he would try to get some sleep so that his brain and nerves would be working well when he stood his ground tomorrow morning.

As he stared up at the stars and listened to his roan gelding stomp and fidget, Longarm wondered if he had finally come to the end of his string. Maybe Gassy was right and he didn't stand a chance tomorrow.

Well, he would just have to see what the day would bring and take his slim chances. One thing was for sure, if push came to shove, he wouldn't hesitate to shoot that fat and corrupt town mayor as well as Captain Norman in less than a heartbeat.

Chapter 16

The moon was high and it was nearing midnight when Longarm was awakened suddenly by the touch of a hand on his face. Startled, he lunged for his revolver, but Donita Ramirez had already moved it out of reach.

"It is me," she said quietly. "I have come to talk to you alone."

Longarm sat up. "You shouldn't sneak up on a man like that. I might have drawn my gun and shot you."

"That's why I moved the gun." Donita sat down beside his bedroll, crossed her legs and laid her elbows on her knees. Cradling her chin in her hands she said, "Your friend Gassy found me last evening and told me of your foolish plan to try to stop the miners from completing their diversion dam. Is this true?"

"Yes," Longarm said, rubbing sleep from his eyes. "I told the mayor of Canyon City and a few of his cronies that the dam construction work had to be halted until some fair settlement could be reached between the Apache and the whites."

"And he would not do that."

"No," Longarm said. "He even said that Captain

131

Norman and his soldiers would make sure that I did not interrupt the work."

Donita nodded. "This does not surprise me."

"Why do your father and his Apache friends work for the army?"

"Sometimes it is better to sleep with the enemy to know his strengths and weaknesses."

"Is this diversion dam almost completed?" Longarm asked. "I saw it only from a distance."

"Yes," Donita told him. "It will soon be finished and then we will have no more water on the reservation. This is what the people of Canyon City want. They would like my people to starve and then be moved so that the reservation is no more. They want to prospect it for more gold."

"I see."

Donita looked up at the stars. "Can I trust you?"

"Yes."

Her eyes fell on him. "Then I will tell you that I am in Canyon City trying to find evidence that I can use against the mayor and the others. Also, I keep my father and our people aware of what is being planned against them."

"So, you're a spy."

Donita shrugged. "I am trying to save my people in the only way that I know how."

"When the diversion dam is completed what good will your spying do the Apache?"

"It will *never* be completed."

Donita said this with such firm conviction that Longarm realized that the Apache must be planning to destroy the dam. "Donita," he said, "if you try to destroy that dam, then the people of Canyon City as well as the United States army will come against the Apache. There is no way that you can win that fight."

She shrugged. "Without the water we would all die anyway. This is our homeland and we have decided to die fighting."

Longarm nodded his head with understanding. "Do you know anything about who killed and scalped the five white miners?"

"I know it was not Apache. I am sure that it was whites sent out to that camp by Mayor Watson and his friends. They want to make the town angry enough to attack us on the reservation."

"What a mess this is," Longarm said, shaking his head.

Donita nodded in agreement. "Will you fight for us?"

"I will if I must."

"You are a good man and a brave man," she said with a sad smile. "But tomorrow you will probably die."

"That's what I keep hearing."

"There is something important you should know," Donita said. "Many years ago . . . before I was born . . . a white man came to this land alone to write and make drawings. He said he was the son of an important man and that his name was John Stanton."

Longarm didn't understand where this was leading. "So? What was he doing here?"

"When my father captured him and was ready to put John Stanton to death for trespassing on this land, he showed my father a book that had pictures of trains and many drawings. He said that he wanted to write such a book about this country and that he thought it would help my people with the whites. My father let this man live and he stayed for several years. John Stanton did many drawings of everything he saw and became a friend of the Apache, but then he went away."

"Yes, but . . ."

Donita quieted him. "In these pictures Stanton drew our people, yes, but also these mountains, valleys and the streams. His drawings would prove that the water of what the whites call Canyon Creek *always* flowed through our reservation."

Longarm suddenly saw what she was driving at. "Did you or your people ever *see* this book that John Stanton wrote?"

"No," she said, "but I am sure that it could be found. The drawings would be thirty or more years old. They would prove that we are telling the truth about the water, is this not so?"

"It is so!"

"Then you should find this book and show it to the people who sent you out here to seek justice."

"You're right," he told her. "And I wonder if John Stanton himself is still alive."

"I have heard that he lives in a place called Prescott."

"I've been there."

"If you found this man he might still be a friend of the Apache and tell the truth about the water."

"Yes," Longarm said. "I think there is an army post at Prescott called Fort Whipple. Prescott is now Arizona's territorial capitol."

"How far is this place?"

Longarm thought about it for a moment. "It is about sixty miles southwest of Sedona. I could go there and be back in ten, maybe twelve days."

"Then perhaps that is where you should go."

"I'll give it some thought," he told her.

"It would be better for you to go to that town and find John Stanton than to go to the dam and be killed tomorrow morning."

"You may be right."

Donita began to undress. "If you are going to help my people, then I will give you all that I have of myself tonight."

Longarm looked up at the moon and stars and smiled. "Sure, senorita, whatever you say."

He rolled over on his side and their lips met. Donita was a beautiful woman and Longarm had no trouble becoming aroused as they kissed and his hands roamed over her lovely body. Her breath began to come faster when his lips tasted her breasts and then she climbed on Longarm and lowered herself to his body.

"You are very big for a white man."

He laughed right out loud. "I take that as a compliment. And you are very beautiful."

Donita sighed with pleasure and impaled herself on his stiff rod. Then, she began to slowly rotate her narrow hips around and around. Longarm had not had a woman since coming out to Arizona on the train and he had to struggle to maintain his self control, so he thought about fishing. But that didn't work very well, so he thought about all the troubles he faced in the morning. And, while those troubles were considerable, within about ten minutes all he could think of was the woman that was stirring her soup with his big spoon.

"You have many scars," Donita panted, rising up a little to study his torso. "You must have fought many battles."

"I have."

"And had many women."

"A few," he said modestly. "But right now you're the only woman on my mind."

"I am glad." She kissed his mouth and rubbed her chest against his chest. "This is good, huh?"

"Better than good," Longarm panted, gripping her hard buttocks and pulling her even harder down upon his tool.

Donita moaned and closed her eyes. In the faint firelight she looked almost like a goddess because her dark skin glistened with perspiration. She started to move faster and faster which excited Longarm beyond his ability to reason.

"Come on," he whispered passionately in her ear. "I want this to be as much for you as for me."

"You still talk too much," she gasped. And then suddenly, her body went wild with gyrations and her hips clenched his manhood and milked every drop of seed that Longarm possessed.

When she stopped shuddering and fell to the side, Longarm pulled out of her and smiled. "I think that you have rewarded my bravery very well, Donita. And if I should be so fortunate as to live beyond tomorrow morning, I will want to repeat what we did tonight."

"And so will I," she told him. "But you should leave for Prescott in the morning to go find John Stanton."

"I don't think I can do that," he told her. "I told the mayor and the others that I'd stop them at the dam and I'm a man who does not go back on his word."

"Maybe you won't have to," she said.

Longarm didn't know what that meant as he lay back and fell asleep.

* * *

Longarm awoke sometime before dawn to the sound of a muffled explosion. He heard gunfire and shouting from the direction of Canyon City.

"Donita!"

She was gone. And, he knew, so was the Canyon Creek diversion dam because Mankiller and the Apache had just blown it all to hell.

Chapter 17

Longarm rode hard for Prescott, all the time wondering if the people of Canyon City had attacked the Apache out of revenge for destroying their diversion dam.

When he reached the territorial capitol four days later he immediately went to the town's newspaper and asked the editor if he knew a John Stanton.

"Of course! He's one of our most illustrious and favored citizens. Mr. Stanton has been the mayor of our fair city three separate times and he could have been territorial governor had he wished. But he's a scholarly and retiring fellow and his health is not nearly what it was. He used to travel a great deal, but he doesn't anymore since Mrs. Stanton passed away two years ago."

"Are you aware of a book that he wrote about the San Carlos Reservation and the Apache Indians?"

"Why of course! It's one of my favorites. I believe it is now in its sixth or seventh printing and still quite popular."

Longarm said, "You wouldn't happen to have a copy, would you?"

"I certainly do. And it's autographed. Why? Are you interested in that area?"

"I am," Longarm told the friendly newspaper editor. "Could I examine your book for a few moments, please?"

"Yes. I'll be right back."

The editor disappeared into another office while Longarm paced nervously. It seemed to take the man a good deal of time, but when he returned it he held the book lovingly in both hands. "As you can see, it's very worn. It's a first edition. I've read this work several times and loaned it to many of my friends . . . but don't tell Mr. Stanton that."

"Why not?"

"Because he'd want them to buy their *own* copies!" the editor said with a laugh.

"Sure, why not. Do you mind if I look through this a few minutes in private?"

"Of course not. Use that copy room next door and I'll see that you are not disturbed."

"Thank you."

It took Longarm fewer than five minutes to find a reference to Canyon Creek, describing in detail the original course it ran south right through the present day reservation. Not only was the description complete, leaving no doubt as to the original watercourse, but there were several excellent drawings that had been reproduced to show Canyon Creek.

"This is it!" Longarm said with satisfaction. "Indisputable proof that the creek has always flowed across the Indians' reservation."

Longarm was more than delighted and relieved by this historic proof that would end the controversy in favor of the Apache.

"If you want your own copy you'll have to buy it from Mr. Stanton," the editor told him. "It's ten dollars, but worth every penny if you are a serious student of Arizona history."

"I am now," Longarm said. "Where can I find the author so that I can buy an autographed copy?"

The editor told Longarm that John Stanton lived just off Prescott's Whiskey Row in a fine Victorian home and gave him excellent directions. "Once you start talking to John and he sees that you're real history buff, you'll have a hard time leaving his house. You know, Mr. Stanton knew Cochise and Geronimo."

"I'm sure he did."

Longarm wasted no time in finding the Stanton home. John Stanton himself opened the door and he was a handsome old gentleman who had once stood over six feet tall, although the years had bent him somewhat. His hair was silver and his bearing was one of intelligence and dignity.

When Longarm sat in the old man's parlor and told him the urgent nature of his visit, John Stanton said, "I should return to Canyon Creek with you and set this matter right. There is no doubt that the creek ran down through what is now the San Carlos Reservation. To think otherwise is either self-serving nonsense or pure ignorance."

"Both, I'm afraid. But Mr. Stanton, it's a long, hard ride to that area, as you well know, and I have to travel fast. Perhaps you could simply write two letters stating what you have told me and what I've seen in your book."

"Why two?"

Longarm explained that he would like to have one of the letters and a book in his possession when he returned to Canyon City, but the other letter along with a book should be sent to his boss, Billy Vail, in Denver. He ended up saying, "Mr. Vail will forward your letter and book to the proper authorities in Washington D.C. so that this dispute can be put to rest once and for all."

"I will be happy to do that." Stanton smiled. "I understand that Geronimo is at the San Carlos Reservation, but that he is unhappy. You know what that means, don't you Marshal Long?"

"I hope it doesn't mean what I think it means."

Stanton shrugged. "Geronimo will bolt the reservation and raise some hell before his time is finished, and you can quote me on that."

"It would be better if he waited until this water issue is settled peacefully," Longarm said. "Things are complicated enough. I got the impression that the San Carlos Reservation is being looted by a Captain Norman. I am quite sure he is working with the officials in Canyon City and that the last thing he wants to do is to help the Apache."

"How unjust!"

"Yes, isn't it."

Stanton steepled his long, bent fingers and thought a moment before saying, "Marshal Long, I know some very important people in Washington D.C. Would it help if I let your feelings about Captain Norman be known among higher ups in the United States army?"

"It would help a great deal," Longarm told the old gentleman. "If the reservation Indians could get a fair shake then they just might not go on the warpath and a lot of lives could be saved on both sides."

"There is a telegraph office here and I'll personally see that the right ears are bent in this matter this very afternoon. And I'll also send a copy of my book and a covering letter to your superior in Denver."

Longarm reached for his wallet and the twenty dollars he would pay for two copies.

"No, don't be silly," Stanton protested. "What you are doing is trying to right a wrong and avoid bloodshed. I could not possibly profit from that effort so the books are free."

Longarm was pleased. Twenty dollars right now was important. "I don't suppose you would throw in your autograph for free on the copy I'll take back to Canyon City?"

"Of course I would!" Stanton cried, clapping Longarm on the shoulder and reaching for his ink pen.

Longarm traded the worn out roan gelding for a young bay gelding and he left Prescott that very same afternoon armed with both a copy of John Stanton's historical work and a letter from the gentleman himself that made it clear where Canyon Creek had always flowed.

If I'm lucky and things didn't already blow up in Canyon Creek, Longarm thought as he galloped out of the territorial capitol and then through some towering red rocks, *this just ought to settle the issue once and for all.*

And as a little icing on the cake, he expected that Senorita Donita Ramirez would be pleased enough to show him her special brand of love and gratitude.

Chapter 18

Longarm was bone-tired from his long journey when he finally returned to Canyon City. He arrived in the mining town after midnight and turned his bay into one of Potter's corrals then pitched it a pile of good grass hay. Not wanting to announce his presence and needing a few hours of uninterrupted sleep, he bedded down in an empty barn stall filled with fresh straw.

The sun was well up and filtering through the cracks in the board walls when Potter finally noticed Longarm.

"Hey, what are you doing sleeping in that stall? This ain't a damned hotel!"

Longarm forced his eyes open and yawned. "I rode in early this morning. I figured you wouldn't want me to wake you up."

"You figured that right. Is that your bay gelding out in my corral?"

"Yep."

"Then you owe me," Potter said, actually sticking out his hand palm upturned.

Longarm pushed himself to his feet. "Put it on my bill," he said as he picked up his rifle and gear, then walked over to a horse trough and dunked his head in the cold water. He had ridden over three hundred miles of mountain trails going to Prescott and back and his butt was sore and his bones ached.

"I always demand payment up front," Potter stated.

Longarm hadn't liked City Councilman George Potter from the moment he'd first laid eyes upon him and so he dropped his belongings and grabbed Potter by the front of his dirty shirt and swung him off his feet, dropping him in his own water trough. Potter let out a bellow and Longarm pushed him under the water and held him there about a minute until the stableman's eyes were bugging with unbridled panic.

Potter came up spitting and gasping for air and Longarm yelled in his face. "Have you found any manners yet?"

"Gawdamn you!" Potter choked, trying to tear free of Longarm's grip, "I'm gonna . . ."

Longarm sent him down under the water again. The man's legs were kicking and he had grasped Longarm's wrists in a desperate attempt to break the hold, but Longarm's grip was much too strong. This time, Potter was down for over a minute and when the man let out a silent scream and started to suck in water, Longarm yanked him out and bent him over the side of the trough.

"Ahhhh!"

Longarm slammed his fist down hard between the drowning man's shoulder blades and Potter heaved up a stream of water. Longarm wondered if he'd gone a little too far as the stableman struggled to clear his lungs and to breathe.

"Don't panic. Just breathe," Longarm said, giving

Potter a few more hard jolts in the back. "Have you found your manners yet, George?"

"Yes!" came a strangled cry. "Oh, please don't do that to me anymore."

"I won't," Longarm promised, "but you're going to tell me everything I want to know about your mayor and town council."

"I . . . I don't know anything!"

"Sure you do, George. The mayor told me that you were on the city council and I'll bet you're all in this water trouble together. You found some government hack that has probably been either fired or retired and he concocted a phony survey report that you people think will stand up in court and rob the San Carlos Reservation of its only source of water. Now isn't that so?"

"No!"

Longarm gave the livery owner a chilling smile and drove him back under the water. By now, Potter was about half dead so Longarm didn't hold him under as long as before. Even so, when he pulled Potter up again, the man's face was gray and he was barely breathing.

"Your last chance, George. Fess up about that surveyor's report or I'll drown you for sure."

"All right! All right!" the man choked as he rolled to the ground, coughing, heaving, and spitting. "*Please* don't do that to me again. I'll go mad if I don't drown first."

Longarm looked around the livery and was glad to see that there were no witnesses. "George," he said, grabbing the liveryman by the collar and dragging him into the barn, "you and I are going to have a nice, long conversation and you're going to tell me *everything* you know about the mayor, Captain Norman and this town's thieves, including yourself, who call themselves city councilmen. Is that understood?"

Potter barely had the strength to nod his head. Longarm dragged the man into the same stall that he'd used to bed down in last night and rolled him over on his back.

"George, you had better start talkin' or you're going to get another hard dunkin' and I don't know for sure that you could take it or not."

"Now start by telling me who this government surveyor is and where I can get a copy of his report."

"His name is Peter Miller and he lives in town. He's got the original, but there are copies."

"Who has those?"

"The mayor and Captain Norman."

"How much was the surveyor paid to draw up this phony report saying that the Apache changed the water course?"

"Two hundred dollars."

"Keep talking."

"There's nothing more to say!" Potter cried. "This town needs that water to stay off the reservation. And there is an old water course."

"Yeah, and it was probably created a couple hundred, if not a thousand years ago, long before the white man came into this country looking for fur and then gold."

"What are you going to do?"

"I have evidence in my saddlebags that proves that the water flowed onto the reservation. There's a man named John Stanton who wrote a book with drawings that prove what I'm saying."

"I've heard of him. Is he still alive?"

"You bet he is," Longarm said.

"So what happens now?" Potter wheezed. "If I turn against them they'll kill me."

"If you don't swear under oath what you've just told me to a judge then *I'll* kill you."

Potter whimpered pitifully. "I don't deserve this!"

"Deserve has nothing to do with it," Longarm told the wet and bedraggled liveryman. "You signed on to deceive and cheat the Apache and now you're going to suffer the consequences. However, if you cooperate fully, I'll see that you don't go to prison nearly as long as the others."

Suddenly, from behind him, a voice said, "Oh, I wouldn't worry about that, George."

Longarm whirled around, hand reaching for his gun. But it was too late. He was facing the mayor and two other men who had their guns trained on him.

"Watson," Longarm said, "this rigged game is up."

The fat man shrugged his round shoulders and smiled. "I agree. But not in the way that you had hoped. Now lift your hands away from that gunbelt and do it real slow."

Longarm knew that it would be suicidal to try to make a play with three pistols pointed at his heart.

"George, take the marshal's gun from his belt, then search him for any other weapons he might have hidden."

"My pleasure," the liveryman said. He searched Longarm overlooking his hideout gun attached to his watch fob. "He's clean."

"Good." The mayor's triumphant grin widened. "Turn around slow, Marshal."

"No."

"Do it or I'll gun you down where you stand! Do

149

you think anyone in this town gives a damn about you or wants you to stop that creek diversion?"

Longarm could see the man's point. He turned slowly around and the next thing he knew he felt a terrible pain in the back of his head and he was tumbling into darkness.

Chapter 19

Mayor Merle Watson looked at Councilman George Potter and said, "Tie him up, roll him up in a tarp and then get him the hell out of town. Once you're miles away in some lonesome place where no one can hear the sound of your gun I want you to put a bullet or two in his brain and then bury him."

"Me?" Potter took a back step as he turned white with dread. "I don't want to kill a United States marshal! My gawd, if someone found out that I done that I'd surely be hanged!"

"That you would," the mayor said as he went over to Longarm's saddlebags and searched them finding both John Stanton's book and letter. He scanned both and then smiled with satisfaction. "This is a lucky break for us, George. If that marshal would have been smart enough to get this to certain people in authority, we'd have lost Canyon Creek's water for certain."

"Look," Potter said, his clothes still wet and his head still spinning from coming so near to death in his own horse watering trough. "Nobody would have more pleasure than I would to see this marshal die, but . . ."

"But nothing!" the mayor shouted. "Do you think we can turn back now? Just let that marshal regain consciousness and say we're sorry? Of course not! We're in far too deep to turn back and you've got a buckboard and tarps so that you can take the marshal out of town and make sure his body is never recovered."

George wiped his hand nervously across his face. "Up until now, we're only guilty of trying to cheat the Indians out of some water. But, if I do this, we could *all* hang."

"Yeah," the mayor said, "we could and most likely would. But we won't because I probably half killed the marshal when I pistol-whipped him just now and you're going to finish the job. We're wasting precious time, George. Don't turn coward on me because we are all in this far too deep."

The two men exchanged long glances and Potter's eyes were the first to break away. "What about the marshal's bay horse?"

"What about it?"

"It's in my corral!" Potter cried. "Someone might . . ."

"Stop it! The marshal rode in late last night. How many people do you think saw him on that horse? And if they did, would they even connect the two?"

"Probably not," Potter finally conceded.

"Then you get rid of the marshal's body and I'll figure out something to do with the horse."

"If you sell that horse, I want half the money."

Mayor Watson shook his head in disgust. "George, sometimes I think you are the most money-grubbing son of a bitch that ever walked the earth. We're all going to profit by seeing the water diverted off the reservation. We're the ones that have bought up most of the land that Canyon Creek is gonna cross and we're the ones that will make fortunes. Do you understand that?"

"Sure," Potter said, swallowing hard, "but I never thought we'd have to go so far as to murder a federal lawman."

"When you play for big stakes sometimes there are big risks," the mayor said. "Now let's quit jawin'. Load that lawman up and git him the hell out of Canyon City. And I mean way out of Canyon City!"

"All right."

"George, take a shovel and bury the big man deep. We don't want his body to be dug up by varmints and then have someone tie us to his death. That's real important. Do you understand?"

"Couldn't be clearer," George Potter replied.

"Good!" Mayor Watson glanced down at Stanton's book and letter. "I think I'll go burn these right now. Together, we're going to tie up the last of the loose ends. No more marshal and no more federal interference."

"Right," Potter said, studying Longarm's unconscious form. "I just wish that we didn't have to kill a United States marshal."

"We either finish him off or he'd have finished us off, George. Think about that long and hard when you bury him deep."

"I will," George promised. "I'll get started right now. But what if someone comes into the barn while I'm . . ."

"Hmmm," the mayor said, "that's the first intelligent thing you've said today. All right I'll watch the door and you wrap the body up in a tarp and load it into your buckboard; then hitch up a team and clear out of here in a hurry."

Potter nodded his head in agreement and set right to work.

"And don't forget to take a pick and a shovel!" the mayor said.

"No, I won't," Potter promised.

Chapter 20

Senorita Donita Ramirez had been waiting for Longarm to return from Prescott after his visit with John Stanton and had figured out to the day when he should return.

Today was the day, but there was no Marshal Long.

Donita watched the main street carefully all morning and then she went to see George Potter and ask him if the marshal had ridden in and left his horse in the liveryman's care. But when she approached the barn she saw something very strange and that was the big marshal almost drowning Potter. Donita slipped back behind a building trying to understand why this would be happening. And each time she peeked around the corner of the building the marshal was again shoving the liveryman under water.

My heavens, Donita thought, *is he really going to drown that man in his own horse water trough?*

And just when it seemed certain that the marshal was going to kill the liveryman he dragged Potter into his own horse barn and shut the door. Donita did not know what to think of this behavior from a federal officer of the law. But she knew better than to interfere so she remained frozen with indecision until she saw Mayor Watson enter the barn.

She heard sharp words but she was too far away to understand them. And she knew that the mayor and councilman were corrupt officials and no friends of the marshal.

What should she do? What *could* she do?

Senorita Ramirez decided that she had to find out what was going on in George Potter's barn so she slipped around some old wagons and a corral then edged up to the back of the barn and carefully peered through a crack in the wooden wall.

What she saw almost made her cry out in alarm. The marshal was on the dirt floor and he was either dead . . . or unconscious. And then while the mayor watched the front door, Donita saw the liveryman tie the marshal's hands behind his back, wrap his body up in a canvas tarp and then struggle to load it into the back of a buckboard. But the marshal was too heavy for the liveryman to lift so the mayor had to help.

Just before he was finally shoved onto the buckboard, Donita heard the marshal groan and her heart leapt for joy because now she knew that he was not yet dead.

She heard the mayor gasp, "George, get a team and hitch 'em up. I've got things to do and you need to get rid of this body. Hurry up, now!"

Donita's eyes widened with understanding. The mayor and the city councilman were going to kill the marshal!

Donita wished that her father, Mankiller, or one of his trusted friends were near so that they could help, but that was not the case so she knew that the marshal's life depended on her and her alone.

She owned a gun, a slouch hat, men's pants and shirt, and some beaded moccasins that would carry her swiftly on foot for miles. And she would need some water and . . . oh, that was enough.

She ran to her little shack at the edge of town, changed out of her dress and retrieved these important things. The gun was an old Navy Colt revolver that used black powder, but it was accurate and she had shot many rabbits with it when she lived on the reservation as a child. And if she could hit a rabbit . . . she could hit a man.

After tucking her long black hair under her hat, Donita pulled it down tight over her forehead, then bolted out of her shack and hurried down the road. She hid behind some trees and waited for the buckboard to appear. When it did, she waited another ten minutes to make sure that she would not be seen by Potter or anyone else, then she started walking fast in its wake. The liveryman was really pushing his team of two horses hard and Donita soon realized that she could not walk fast enough to keep pace, so she began to trot like a dog or an Apache warrior.

The sky was blue, the air was clean and she felt scared, but never more alive. She passed some wagons and men called out to her probably thinking she was some crazy boy or young man. Senorita Ramirez ignored all of them and kept running. She had no idea where the liveryman was going to take the unconscious marshal, but she would be there when he stopped and she would somehow prevent the marshal from further harm or death.

Donita whispered an Apache prayer and concentrated on her stride. The road was rough but she was surefooted and very strong. Furthermore, there wasn't a single doubt in her mind that she would be able to keep up with the buckboard even if it rolled all the way down to Old Mexico.

Chapter 21

Longarm awoke with a piercing pain in his head and a sense that he was suffocating. He opened his eyes and knew at once that he was wrapped in an old canvas tarp, but when he tried to unwrap himself, he found that his hands were tied behind his back and his feet bound at the ankles.

Longarm began to sweat profusely because he had no doubt that he was in a buckboard wagon going to his own funeral, although he did not know the exact location or time that he would die.

I've got to get out of here, he thought, *for there is no telling how soon this wagon will stop and I'll be killed.*

But knowing he had to escape and actually escaping were two different things and the harder Longarm struggled to free himself the more he became frustrated and out of breath. It was stiflingly hot wrapped in the heavy canvas and he was afraid that if he did not slow down his frenetic exertions, he might suffocate.

So Longarm forced himself to lie still and to focus on what he could do to get himself out of this deadly situation. He thought and quietly struggled with his bonds, but he was wrapped up tighter than a fat woman in a small woman's corset and getting nowhere.

Finally, the wagon stopped and he heard the driver set the brake and felt him climb down to the ground.

Here it comes, Longarm thought. *Someone is going to shoot holes into me without my even being unwrapped. I'll just jerk a few times and then I'll be dragged out of this buckboard like a sack of bad grain and tossed into a ditch or over the side of a cliff.*

I'm finished.

Longarm next heard the sound of a shovel striking hard gravel. A voice he recognized as belonging to George Potter cursed. The shovel banged off another rock with a tinny sound and Longarm felt Potter reach into the buckboard and slide a heavy object along the floor.

Moments later there was more grunting and cussing to the accompaniment of what was unmistakably the sound of a pick now striking the flinty ground.

He's digging my grave and having a tough time of it, Longarm realized as he began to struggle frantically once again with the same futile results. *I'm listening to a man dig my grave and I can't do a damned thing about it.*

Suddenly, the thought struck him that George Potter might just dump him in the grave and bury him *alive*. Cold sweat burst out all over Longarm's body and he wanted to scream yet he knew that any sound he made would hasten his own death.

Then Longarm heard and felt something else. Something very close. Something that was working at the tarp with a cutting tool.

"It is Donita," the voice whispered. "Marshal, I have to get you out of here fast!"

Longarm knew that Donita had to be on the off side of the buckboard away from Potter. She was taking a tremendous chance since he could easily look over and see her feet under the wagon or the top of her head as she struggled to cut Longarm free.

"Donita," he whispered, "do you have a gun?"

"Yes."

"Use it now!"

The cutting of the tarp ceased for a moment and then continued. Clearly, the half-breed woman did not want to shoot George Potter. Instead, she was trying to cut Longarm free so he could defend them both.

"Hey!"

It was Potter's shrill voice and Longarm knew that the liveryman had seen the woman.

"Shoot him or we're both dead!" Longarm shouted into the canvas that bound him like a shroud. "Do it!"

"Hey, what . . . it's you, senorita!"

"Don't move, Mr. Potter." Her voice was filled with anxiety, but Longarm also heard steely resolve. "Don't move or I'll have to shoot."

Potter knew he had to move. "Senorita Ramirez, get away from that buckboard. Come over here."

"No! Put your hands up."

Longarm heard a subtle change in Potter's voice. Now it was more reasonable and coaxing. "Donita, put the gun down and we can talk. We just need to talk."

"Don't come any closer!"

"Now just you listen to me you half-breed bitch!" Potter shouted, anger overcoming his good sense. "Drop that old pistol or I'll take it away from you and . . ."

Whatever Canyon City Councilman George Potter was going to do to Donita ended with the blast of her

161

Navy Colt. Longarm heard Potter cry out in pain and then the sound of his boots coming fast.

"Shoot him again. Shoot for the heart!" Longarm cried, knowing that everything depended on the woman killing Potter.

Two more shots followed in rapid succession and then Longarm heard Potter's body hit the buckboard and the man's dying gasp.

"You . . . you bloody bitch!" he raged.

A sob escaped the woman's mouth and then she grabbed the tarp and jerked it hard.

"Cut me free, senorita," Longarm ordered. "Just cut me free and I'll take care of the rest of it."

"I killed him."

"Of course you did," Longarm said as she uncovered his face and then went around to the other side of the wagon and reached over to cut loose the bonds around his wrists and ankles. "If you hadn't shot him dead, he would have killed the both of us without a moment's hesitation. You did what you had to do to save our lives."

Longarm tumbled out of the wagon, then slowly climbed to his feet and looked over the situation. His ankles had been tied so tightly that both his hands and his feet were numb. As he waited for sensation to return he saw that Potter's buckboard was hidden deep in the forest. Nearby was the half-finished grave and it was about two feet deep cut from rocky ground.

But the main point of interest was George Potter who lay beside his wagon with three bullets in his body, which was now covered with blood. One wound was in the arm, the other in Potter's belly and the third had drilled the liveryman straight through the heart.

"You did just fine," Longarm said, limping over to

Donita and putting his arm around her shoulders, then pulling her close. "You did more than I can ever expect to repay you for."

"I knew that he was going somewhere to bury you," she said. "The only thing I did not know was if you were already dead or not."

"I would have been dead by now if you hadn't followed." Longarm looked around. "Where is your horse?"

"I don't have one. I followed on foot."

Longarm glanced down at her moccasins and at the men's clothing she wore and understood. "I'm thirsty. Is there any water close by?"

"Yes. There is a spring only a little ways back. What about Mr. Potter?"

Longarm turned to look at the body. Potter actually looked at peace. "I'll dig the grave a little deeper and that's where he'll go to a permanent rest," Longarm decided.

"And then what?"

Longarm swallowed dryly. "I don't know, Donita. I'm going to have to return to Canyon City and arrest a lot of men now that I understand what has been going on here."

"But they have the army to help them."

"You mean Captain Norman?"

Donita nodded.

Longarm thought about that a moment and then he said, "Do you know how the people in Africa eat a great big elephant?"

"No."

Longarm forced a smile. "One bite at a time, Donita. One bite at a time."

"What does that mean?

163

"It means that I'll take Mayor Watson down first and then I'll go after the other city councilmen. One by one I'll get them locked up and out of action before Captain Norman or his men know what is going on. Then, when the soldiers come I will figure out some way to arrest . . . or kill them all . . . if I have to."

"One bite at a time," Donita said. "Or one *man* at a time."

"That's right." Longarm kissed her brow. "You are a very fine and brave woman. Your father will be proud of what you have done this day. And maybe he and his friends will help me with the soldiers."

"Maybe," Donita said, looking over at the man she had shot to death. "But we talk too much."

"There are others who might help as well," Longarm thought, remembering Gassy's vow to help him no matter what the odds.

"We should bury this man quickly before someone comes along."

"You're right," Longarm said, scooping up the heavy digging pick. "I'll get right at it."

Donita took the shovel and set to work helping him. Working together, they had greedy George Potter planted in no time at all.

Chapter 22

Longarm and Donita drove the buckboard back to Canyon City arriving unnoticed after dark. They hadn't said much on their return trip and Longarm supposed that the dark-haired beauty who had saved his life was thinking about having to shoot a man. Longarm knew it was always hardest killing for the first time.

"Donita, I'll put the horses away and feed them. We'll just leave the buckboard in the barn."

"What then?"

"I'm going to arrest Mayor Merle Watson, the stud duck in this foul pond called Canyon City. He's as crooked as a snake in a cactus patch. The trouble is I don't know what to do with him because I didn't see anything like a jail in this town."

Donita thought a few moments. "There have been times when they had to jail troublemakers, mostly just drunk people for a night or two. Once, they hanged a man for killing a prostitute."

"Where did they hold these people?"

"There is a small cave at the east end of town."

Longarm wasn't sure that he'd heard correctly. "Did you say a cave?"

"Yes," Donita said. "I have walked past it, but of course never been inside. Someone drilled hinges into the rock and bolted a solid wood door on the cave so the prisoners cannot escape."

"It sounds perfect. Who has the key to this cell in the rock?"

Donita almost smiled. "The mayor?"

Longarm laughed out loud. "Tell me, is the mayor a married or single man?"

"No woman in her right mind would marry that pig. He is also very mean."

Longarm nodded in agreement. "He's a lot more than mean. And Merle Watson is going to prison for a long, long time. It's just that right now I haven't got the time to take him to Yuma. So I'll round the mayor and the other councilmen up and then I'll see that they all go to prison at once. Tell me where he and the other city councilmen live."

Longarm got the directions he needed. Turns out that with George Potter dead, there were only three other councilmen and the mayor.

Donita said, "And what will you do about Captain Norman and his soldiers?"

"Hmmm," Longarm mused, "I do seem to keep overlooking them, don't I? How many soldiers and Apache scouts do you think are loyal to the Captain and will stick with him in a showdown against a federal officer of the law?"

Donita did not have to consider the question for more than a second. "No Apache. Only a few soldiers. One soldier for sure."

"And that would be that big sergeant that Captain Norman keeps chained by his side like an attack dog."

"Yes," she said. "His name is Sergeant Mick Mooney."

"He looks like a Mick," Longarm said. "Big Irishman a little short on brains."

"He likes to beat people up when he gets drunk. He is a bad man in a fight. I have seen what he does to men and some never recover in the head."

"That doesn't surprise me," Longarm replied. "Donita, will you do me another favor?"

"Sure. If I can."

"Find Gassy and tell him to get over to that rock jail and be waiting for the mayor and then the others as I bring them in tonight. As for Captain Norman, I'll figure that one out tomorrow."

"I could go to the reservation and talk to my father. Maybe even Geronimo would help."

Longarm knew he could sure use the help, but on the other hand he was very reluctant to get the San Carlos Apache involved knowing that they would be caught in a huge backlash and severely punished. So, if he could handle this without them, then that would be best.

"I'd rather you kept the Apache out of this mess," he told the woman. "But if I get killed . . ."

"You won't."

"No," he said, seeing worry cloud her pretty face, "I won't."

The senorita left to find Gassy, and Longarm set off to pay a visit to Mayor Watson who lived in a one-room house behind the hotel. When Longarm arrived at the mayor's house, he saw that a light was on inside and he heard a woman's coarse laughter.

Longarm crept up to the little house and peeked in through a dirty window. The mayor was in his underwear and a short, chubby young prostitute was sitting naked on his lap with a bottle of whiskey in her hand. The mayor was playing with the woman's breasts which were sadly only about half the size of his own. The very sight of the pair gave Longarm a stab of intense heartburn or indigestion.

He drew his gun and went up to the door expecting it to open. But the door was locked and he heard the mayor shout, "Who's that at my door?"

Longarm leaned back and kicked the door open tearing it from its rusty hinges. His gun was in his fist and leveled at the couple.

Mayor Watson's jaw dropped. "By gawd, Marshal, what are you . . ."

"You're under arrest," Longarm said cutting him off. "Stand up and put your pecker back in your underwear or I'll shoot that little cob clean off."

"Are you mad?" the prostitute cried. "Merle is the *mayor* of Canyon City."

"*Was* the mayor," Longarm said. "Woman, get dressed and get out of here."

"How dare you!" she cried, trying to muster up some righteous outrage.

Longarm reached into his pocket and produced his badge. "Woman, if you want to go to prison then keep on squawkin.' Otherwise, vamoose!"

The pudgy whore took a pull on the bottle of whiskey, looked down at what she'd spilled and suddenly realized she was naked. In a completely ridiculous gesture, she covered both of her little breasts with her hands and then jumped up and turned her back to Longarm. Longarm's stomach went even more sour because he now had the misfortune of having to look at her backside which was uglier than the south end of a sow and wider than an ore wagon.

"Get your clothes and leave!" Longarm shouted.

The woman grabbed up her belongings and then started to put them on. She was in such a hurry and so upset that she toppled and fell with one leg in and one leg out of her pantaloons. It was, Longarm thought, one of the most disgusting sights he had ever witnessed while stone sober.

"Go!"

The woman gave up her struggles, gathered up her clothing and charged the door. He heard her cussing and screeching all the way down the road.

"Nice taste you have in women," Longarm said. "About what I would have expected."

"Go *screw* yourself, Marshal!"

"I'd probably try before I'd take on that woman," Longarm said with a shake of his head. "Now grab some clothes and let's get out of here."

"Where are we going?"

"You'll find out when we get there."

"What happened to George Potter?"

"Well," Longarm said, "after you pistol-whipped me and I was taken away in a buckboard to be buried probably alive, I managed to escape. Potter won't be coming back to town again. Ever."

The mayor paled. "You killed him?"

Longarm thought it best to assume that responsibility because the very last thing he wanted was for Donita to be implicated in any way.

"And I'll shoot you, too, if you don't get moving."

"You'll pay for this with your life," Watson vowed. "You'll hang from the highest tree in Canyon City!"

"No," Longarm told the man, "but you'll sweat a lot of that lard off over the years in Yuma Prison. The temperature there in the summer gets so high that candles melt in the shade and fat fellas like you do the same. You're going to be a damned beanpole, so skinny you'll be able to take a shower in a shotgun's barrel."

The mayor swallowed hard and his lower lip began to quiver. "Maybe we should talk. You could get rich if you used some sense. We could cut you into the action."

"No, thanks."

The mayor's eyes narrowed. "You fool! You've no evidence left to fight us in court."

"You'd be talking about John Stanton's book and letter?"

"That's right. I destroyed both."

"It doesn't matter," Longarm said. "I can get more books from Stanton and he'll rewrite his letter. So you and whoever else was in cahoots to steal the reservation's water have lost everything."

"You've signed your own death warrant, Marshal!"

"Shut up and find the key to that hole in the rock wall that you use to jail the town drunks."

"No!" Watson cried. "I won't go there because that's a stinking shit hole."

"Then you'll be right at home. The keys . . . or your little cob turns into a bloody string." Longarm cocked back the hammer of his six-gun and pointed it at the mayor's little pecker to emphasize his words.

Watson jumped and found the key before he found his pants. Fifteen minutes later Longarm prodded the half naked mayor into the rock jail and said to Gassy,

"This is your first customer. If he makes a fuss or starts raisin' Cain, then you have my permission to go inside and shoot Mayor Watson where it does the most good."

"My pleasure," Gassy said as he closed and locked the heavy wooden door, but not before fumigating the cell with his very worst fart. "Marshal, how soon will this one have visitors?"

"They'll be coming as fast as I can round them up," Longarm told his old friend.

"And if someone comes to set the mayor free?"

"Then you have my permission to set that person free . . . permanently free."

"That's all I needed to know," Gassy said with a grin.

Over the next hour Longarm corralled and then jailed the other city councilmen. By then it was almost daybreak and he was feeling woozy and very weary. But he'd done a fine night's work and knew that he was lucky to be alive and for that he had to thank Senorita Donita Ramirez.

He went to her little shack as the sun was peeking over the cliffs and said, "I need to sleep a bit. Can you watch over me for an hour or two? After that, I'll try and come up with some way to arrest Captain Norman and any of his soldiers who get in my way."

"Sit down on the bed and let me look at your head. It looks awful."

"It doesn't feel real good, either."

Longarm sat while Donita examined the place where the barrel of a pistol had impolitely parted his hair. "Ouch!"

"I will heat some water and stitch it."

"It needs stitches?"

"They would help it heal."

"I don't like stitches," Longarm complained. "Just clean it up, put something on it and it'll mend just fine."

"Marshal, you have a very hard head and that is why you are still alive," she said.

"No," he corrected, "*you're* the reason why I'm still alive. And did I thank you?"

"*Si*. I mean yes."

"I will thank you again when this is over. How would you like to be thanked?"

She smiled. "I would like you to stay with me for a few days and then take me to the reservation. And then I would like you to promise Geronimo, my father and the other Apache leaders that they will never again have someone running their reservation like Captain Norman and the sergeant."

"I will tell them that the captain and the sergeant were bad and will not come back. That will be my only promise."

Donita thought for a moment and then she nodded in agreement. "It would be enough of a promise. And we will make love before you go in my bed on the reservation."

"Are you sure that is all right with Mankiller?" Longarm asked, the image of his throat and then his scalp being savaged by a dull and rusty hunting knife.

"Yes. For by then they will know that you are a great warrior and worthy of Mankiller's daughter."

"We're not going to have to get married, are we? No offense, Donita, but I'm not going to be married."

"No marriage. Just . . . you know."

A smile creased Longarm's lips because he *did* know.

For the next twenty minutes he sat patiently as the senorita cleaned his scalp wound and then he lay down on her bed. In a few hours he would try to figure out how he would handle the army. He sincerely hoped that he would not have to shoot Captain Norman and the sergeant. But he would do what was necessary. Longarm realized that he *always* did what was necessary as he fell into a deep and dreamless sleep.

Chapter 23

"Sergeant Mooney!"

"Yes, sir!"

Captain Norman ran his fingers though his thinning brown hair. "I was supposed to hear from Mayor Watson this morning about something very important. But the man hasn't shown up. What do you think might have caused him to be missing?"

Mick Mooney shrugged his wide shoulders. "Beats the hell out of me, Captain. He probably got drunk again with that fat little whore he's so taken with these days. I'm sure he's just sleeping it off."

"Yes," Norman said, "that's probably the case. It's going to be hot today. Very warm."

"Looks like, sir."

"Any trouble this morning when you handed out the week's food rations to Geronimo and his savage crowd?"

"No, sir." Mooney frowned. "But you can tell they're up to something."

The captain looked up suddenly. "What does *that* mean?"

"They just look like they're about to jump the ship . . . I mean the reservation."

"If they do that one more time they will all be captured and shot. So much the better because we won't be stuck here in this miserable hell hole of a reservation any longer."

"My feelings exactly, sir."

The captain tapped his pencil on his desktop in rapid succession. "But I am concerned with the mayor's absence. Take a few men and go into town. Find and bring our degenerate Mayor Watson back to me. That's an order."

"Yes, sir."

"And Sergeant?"

"Yes, sir?"

"Don't even think about stopping at the whorehouse or the saloon. I want you and your soldiers to be back here this afternoon with Watson. Is that clearly understood?"

"Oh, yes, sir!"

"Good. Then you are dismissed."

Sergeant Mick Mooney *would* pay a quick visit to the whorehouse and the saloon. And he'd buy a bottle of cheap whiskey to bring back for tonight. But he'd also find and deliver that little rat, Mayor Watson.

As he stepped out of the headquarters office and looked up at the sky he decided that the day might not be quite as hot as yesterday. And he would have a whole lot more fun going into town than sitting here on this miserable, stinking reservation.

It was early afternoon when Donita awakened Longarm with no small amount of urgency. "Marshal, wake up! The sergeant and two of his men are in town looking for the mayor. Someone will know where they are and the soldiers will go to the rock jail and turn everyone loose."

Longarm groaned and rolled off Donita's bed. He checked his gun and then said, "Where can I borrow a double-barreled shotgun and a handful of shells?"

"I know a man who has those things."

"Please go get them and come back as fast as you can," Longarm told her as he rolled off the bed and then staggered over to a basin of cool water so that he could bathe his face and clear his mind.

The man that Donita knew must have lived nearby because she returned in minutes with the shotgun as well as four shells. Longarm would have preferred more shells, but he figured that these, along with his sidearm, would be sufficient to do what was necessary.

Longarm loaded the shotgun noting that it was quite old, poorly made and not in especially good condition. Yet, he had no doubt that the weapon would fire and deal a spray of death should the sergeant and his men force the issue to the limit.

Longarm gently screwed down his hat, checked his own gun and then loaded two shells into the shotgun. "I'll be back before long," he said to the woman. "Just wait here and everything will turn out all right."

Donita shook her head. "I can shoot. You know that I can shoot and I want to come with you."

"Thanks for the offer, but you've done more than enough for me already. Just stay here and wait."

Donita kissed his mouth. "If you are killed, I swear that I will get my gun and kill the sergeant even if it costs me my life."

Longarm looked into her eyes and wanted to tell Donita that she should not do such a thing, but he knew that he would be wasting both time and words. So he just nodded and left her shack.

He approached the rock cell in a roundabout manner and hid behind a tree until he saw that Gassy was still guarding the cell and had not been disturbed.

Longarm went to the old prospector and said, "No trouble?"

"Not yet, but I understand that big sergeant is in town asking for the mayor. Someone is bound to know we've got him and the other council members locked up in this cell. The sergeant will be around soon enough."

"Yeah, I expect so."

"What . . ."

Longarm cut Gassy off in mid-sentence. "I'll try to talk the sergeant into giving up his gun. If he doesn't . . . then I'll have to take it from him."

"He won't give up anything to you," Gassy said. "Sergeant Mooney will fight to the death."

"I expect you are right." Longarm heard a voice and then he turned and said, "Here they come now."

"There's only three of them," Gassy said. "And you're holding a shotgun. I don't think even the sergeant is stupid enough to buck us."

"We'll see."

When the sergeant saw Longarm and Gassy standing beside the heavy wooden door he reined up his horse and said, "I understand that you have the mayor and the whole city council locked up in that cave."

"Not all of them," Longarm replied. "I killed George Potter yesterday."

Sergeant Mooney blinked and when he recovered, said, "I'm going to have to arrest you."

"You got it backward," Longarm told the big soldier. "Get off your horse and hand over your gun so that you and your men can live to fight another day."

Mooney stared at Longarm and then finally dismounted. "If you kill me or any of my men there is nothing that will keep you from hanging."

"You'll never know because you'll be resting six feet under the ground."

"Marshal, drop that shotgun."

"Sergeant, you're under arrest. Your two men can escort me back to the reservation post, but you're going into this rock cell with the other scum."

Mooney's jaw tightened. "The hell you say because I won't do it."

Longarm raised the shotgun and started marching toward the sergeant. "Don't make me kill you. I can't miss at this range."

Mooney was suddenly very afraid. Longarm could see fear in the big Irishman's eyes and yet the man did not back down. For the briefest instant, Longarm considered shooting the fool and then he decided not to.

"Mooney, throw your best punch at me," Longarm said, coming up to arms length of the sergeant.

"Huh?"

"Swing! Try and knock my head off."

Mooney finally got it and he threw a straight right hand that Longarm sidestepped as he lashed out with the shotgun and bent over Mooney's stone hard head. The Irishman went down like a ton of rocks.

"Gassy, put him in the jail cave with the others."

"I'll need help," the old prospector said. "He's even bigger than Potter's barn."

"Boys," Longarm said, addressing the two shocked soldiers, "dismount and help my friend."

The two soldiers were young. Mere privates. They

hesitated until Longarm waved the bent barrel of the shotgun at them and then they jumped off their mounts and gave Gassy a hand.

Donita came hurrying over to Longarm. "You almost have them all," she said. "Like they eat an elephant in Africa."

"Yes, one bite at a time."

"Now you must get Captain Norman."

"Will you ride down to your reservation with me?"

She nodded, eyes shining brightly. "Will you have to kill the captain?"

"No," Longarm said after a moment's thought. "With all of his corrupt cronies arrested and his sergeant joining them in that cave jail, I'm pretty sure that Captain Norman will surrender without a fight."

"Then you take him for a coward."

"Yes," Longarm said, "I'm sure of it."

Late that day Longarm and Donita rode together up to the army headquarters where Captain Norman was waiting. Mankiller and another Apache leader that Longarm thought might be Geronimo were among the Indians who came to watch. None of them said anything as Longarm dismounted and handed his reins to Donita.

"This won't take long," he told the half-breed woman.

Captain Norman was standing by his office desk with a gun clenched in his fist. In a strained voice that betrayed his anxiety, he said, "You're under arrest, Marshal."

Longarm put his hand on the butt of his pistol. "That's the second time I've heard that said today. First from your man Mooney, now from you. Captain, the mayor and his henchmen along with your sergeant are locked up and under my arrest. I have proof positive that the Apache have legal claim to Canyon Creek so you're not going to profit even a penny."

"What proof?"

"A book with drawings made by a very prominent gentleman who mapped the river's flow long before you came into the picture."

The captain's shoulders seemed to droop and all this false bravado faded. "You seem to have it all figured out, don't you, Marshal?"

"Pretty much," Longarm said almost matter-of-factly. "Captain, your fate rests squarely in your own hands. You can join your friends that I've already arrested . . . or you can die here and now."

A tic formed at the corner of Norman's mouth and the gun in his hand began to shake. "I'm holding the gun, in case you haven't noticed."

"Oh," Longarm said, "I've noticed. But in case you haven't noticed, Geronimo, Mankiller and a whole bunch of other Apache warriors are outside. I'm sure that they're listening and waiting to see what will happen next."

"What will happen is that I will kill you!" Norman said, raising the gun and pointing it at Longarm.

"And what do you think they will do to you in repayment, Captain? Kiss your ass in gratitude? Nope. They'll skin you alive and you'll die strangling in your own blood and howling like a scalded dog. Is that the way you want your miserable, greedy life to end?"

Norman turned white. "No," he managed to wheeze.

"Then drop the gun and you'll be under my arrest and protection. I'll take you back to Canyon City and then on to the Yuma Prison with the others."

"The *Yuma* Prison?"

"That's right. But I'm sure that you'll be paroled . . . in about fifty years."

"I've heard of the Yuma Prison," Norman said, his eyes unfocused and wide with panic. "I wouldn't survive there. Not for even a year."

"I can't help you about that, Captain. Now hand over the gun or I'll send the Apache in here to deal you their brand of justice."

The gun in Captain Norman's hand began to shake violently and then he suddenly jerked it up and jammed the barrel into his mouth.

Longarm knew what the captain was doing and he didn't move to prevent it as Norman blew out his brains.

Donita came running. She barged into the headquarters and skidded to a stop. "What?"

"Captain Norman didn't like the choices I gave him," Longarm said, turning to the woman and then leading her back outside. "And you know what?"

"What?" she managed to ask.

"Probably for the first time in his life he did the right thing."

Longarm looked out across the compound at the crowd of Apache warriors. *Yep*, he thought, *that is definitely Geronimo standing beside Mankiller. Maybe I averted another Apache War by setting this right.*

Longarm took a deep breath and raised his hand palm outward toward the famous Geronimo and then he nodded as if to tell the great warrior that justice had at last been served.

Geronimo slowly raised his own hand in a sign of

182

peace and understanding. Their eyes met across the
dusty compound and Longarm had the feeling that, in
addition to saving a lot of lives, he might even have
changed some Arizona history.

Watch for

**LONGARM AND THE
FALSE PROPHET**

the 331st novel in the exciting LONGARM
series from Jove

Coming in June!

LONGARM

**Explore the exciting Old West with one
of the men who made it wild!**

GIANT-SIZED ADVENTURE FROM AVENGING ANGEL LONGARM.

LONGARM AND THE UNDERCOVER MOUNTIE
0-515-14017-1

THIS ALL-NEW, GIANT-SIZED ADVENTURE IN THE POPULAR ALL-ACTION SERIES PUTS THE "WILD" BACK IN THE WILD WEST.

U.S. MARSHAL CUSTIS LONG AND ROYAL CANADIAN MOUNTIE SEARGEANT FOSTER HAVE AN EVIL TOWN TO CLEAN UP—WHERE OUTLAWS INDULGE THEIR WICKED WAYS. BUT FIRST, THEY'LL HAVE TO STAY AHEAD OF THE MEANEST VIGILANTE COMMITTEE ANYBODY EVER RAN FROM.

J. R. ROBERTS

THE GUNSMITH